The Young and the Reckless

RED BUD AVE
Publications

CHECK OUT OTHER TITLES BY RED BUD AVE PUBLICATIONS

TAYLOR MADE
SIMPLY TAYLOR MADE
WASHED UP
TALES FROM THE LOU
DIAMONDS ARE TRULY FOREVER (E-book)
MISPLACED LOYALTY
NO LIMIT

Copyright © 2019 Teresa Seals
Published by Red Bud Ave Publications, LLC

Sale of this book without a front cover may be unauthorized. If this book is without a cover, it may have been reported to the publisher as *unsold or destroyed* and neither author nor the publisher may have received payment for it.

All rights reserved. No part of this book may be reproduced, stored in or introduced into a retrieval system, or transmitted, in any form or by any means electronic, mechanical, photocopying, recording or otherwise, without prior written permission of both the copyright owner and the publisher of this book.

Publisher's Note:
This is a work of fiction. Any names to historical events, real people, living and dead, or to real locales are intended only to give the fiction a setting in historic reality. Other names, characters, places, business and incidents are either the product of the author's imagination or are used fictitiously, and their resemblance, if any, to real life counterparts is entirely coincidental.
Library of Congress Catalog No.: Pending

ISBN 10: 0-9844397-5-7
ISBN 13: 978-0-9844397-5-1
Cover Design: Robert Ford, Jr.
Editor: Jon B. King
FIRST EDITION

Printed in the United States of America

The Young and the Reckless

CHAPTER 1

Shortly after midnight, the menacing sounds of the March winds maneuvered meticulously through the streets of the Midwest. Pitter patter, pitter patter was the rhythm of the falling rain which was in sync with the howling wind and the rumbling thunder were the only sounds that could be heard. The condensation which emerged from the darkness of several roofs were racing throughout the atmosphere in a smoky mist. Small puffs of smoke could be seen from every home that dwelled upon the city streets.

The clock struck three and not a creature was stirring, the raining tornado weather had come through the city's northside like a thief in the night. Various forms of debris floated spontaneously through the air. The moonlight was tucked away in the clouds. The moon appeared to be lost in the galaxy.

Hustlers who hustled in rain, sleet and snow, that could sell water to a whale, weren't even roaming about. The streets were empty during this spring night as the temperatures were quite frigid, and the strong downburst was severe. The vacant streets were as though it was one of those harsh winter nights where hypothermia could set in. The emptiness of the outdoors suggested that all the citizens that usually flooded the streets were aware of the consequences on this maliciously type of night.

    "This is my last time asking yo ass!" The tall masked man dressed in all black like the omen spoke with a distinctive firm authoritative tone. He continued to speak enunciating each word slowly ensuring that his demands were being understood very clearly, "You need to open this safe right now or this situation may not end well for you, Bruh!" The masked man barked his demand ferociously as he gripped tightly to the black Smith and Wesson placing it directly towards the dome of Xavier's head. The masked man looked down on Xavier and could see the fear in his eyes as he kneeled on the side of his king size bed in front of a custom made safe, he was demanding to be opened. Xavier attempted to tilt his head to look toward the masked man, praying he could see the sincerity in his eyes.

    Boom! The loud sound of the thunder startled them all. Xavier didn't want to make direct eye contact with the intruder which could possibly be perceived in the wrong way. He had no clue to how his current predicament would end but he hoped for the best. He just didn't want it to be a tragic one. The merciless look in the eyes of the masked man that was hoisted over him gave him a sinister feeling. He feared his wife waking up to two unknown individuals standing in their bedroom, demanding he open a safe that she didn't know or even agree with being there in the first place. Xavier was wrapping his mind around the situation and began to realize

The Young and the Reckless

that his current quandary may not end well for him and his wife.

Xavier glanced up at the clock that sat on top of the safe that was designed to look as if it were a very expensive nightstand. Only on the surface, the African Blackwood revealed its elegance. Hand engraved floral work that resembled a henna design were along the edges and on the top were four small roaring lions engraved in each corner. The African Blackwood covered up a ten cubic feet electronic safe that contained a monetary amount close to a million dollars. In their bedroom were two identical nightstands. Only one of the nightstands doors could be opened and utilized. The other nightstand was just fraudulent. The door and handle were imposters on the nightstand, Xavier was currently knelt before the nightstand as though he was on a Janamaz pointed toward Mecca. This nightstand only opened from the top. As soon as it opened the electronic keypad was there waiting for someone to enter the magic four-digit pin code.

The alarm clock boldly read 3:14. When Xavier noticed the time, he knew his daughter Nevaeh would be coming in their bedroom in under fifteen minutes, to climb in their bed and his son Cinque would be sure to follow. At the age of eight, Nevaeh was still being bribed to sleep in her own bed. Xavier and his wife would get her to fall asleep in her own room, but she couldn't make it through the entire night all alone. Like clockwork she would show up at 3:29 in her parent's bedroom. Xavier thought it was very ironic that she was born March twenty-ninth and she came into their bedroom every morning at that same time consistently. Neveah's arrival time was a constant reminder of her date of birth.

    Xavier knew Cinque would be right behind Neveah as if he knew that he needed to cherish every moment he had with his mother and father. He smiled in amazement thinking about how his ten-year-old son still craved for his attention as if he were the same three-year-old that followed up behind him, moving every time he did. Xavier admired how Cinque mimicked just about everything he did, right down to him placing his right pointer finger on the front of his lips when he was in deep thought to him twisting his mouth to the far left as though he was chewing when he was wrapping up his thoughts or coming to a resolution of whatever he was thinking about. He cherished every moment he had with Cinque because the first six months of his life he was housed in neonatal incubator. His wife had to have an emergency caesarean section due to her experiencing a placental abruption. Xavier thought about the first day he held his son and his smile quickly became a frown as he knew he needed to end this life or death soon.

    Xavier didn't want to make the wrong move. He was kneeling on the floor with a gun pointed directly to his head. He had heard stories about being held at gun point but never experienced it himself. His blood was boiling with anger but fear clearly had him deciding to make wise choices in resolving his present dilemma. He felt so violated. Some individuals had the audacity to come into his sacred domain. The place where he sat down to

The Young and the Reckless

have family dinners and nurtured his children. Now two masked men stood in the same room he made sweet tender love to his wife. He made the decision to plead his case, "Look, man, my kids are in the next room and I don't want any problems. What can I do besides open this safe to help you understand that I don't know the code to this safe? It belongs to my brother. I honestly don't know the combination." Xavier spoke nervously as he looked up, trying to avoid making direct eye contact with the intruder, to see if he was about to be sympathetic with him as he tried to plead his case. When he noticed there was no change in the man's disposition, he continued, "Look my man; I can get the combination to the safe. Just give me a minute to call my brother. I promise I'll just ask him the combination as though it's something I need out of it that can't wait. I don't have any ulterior motives. I'll make the phone call, get the combination and that will be it."

Xavier was pissed at himself. He was supposed to have gotten a panic button installed on the safe. It would have alarmed the authorities and his alarm company. He was trying to avoid Bria being aware of the safe but deep down inside he knew she was not going to say anything to him about it. She took her wedding vows seriously. She was the epitome of honoring thy husband. Xavier had done all things except walk on water to make her feel appreciated. He let her know her worth along with establishing a lifestyle for her to be the submissive wife that she was.

The masked man contemplated on allowing him to make the phone call to get the combination to the safe. He didn't know how much money was in the safe, but he figured that the man he was attempting to rob had touched more than 10 million dollars in the last four years, so the home invasion was worth it. He knew Xavier's brother had a nice run in the dope game. Everyone comp'd work from Xavier's brother Pharaoh. The robber didn't know if Xavier was in the family business or not. At this point he didn't care. He knew he could walk away a very wealthy individual once the safe was opened.

The tears began to slowly fall upon his face, Xavier thought we would be shown some sympathy from the other masked individual who hadn't uttered a word. He stood stationery over his wife with the weapon pointed. Xavier would sporadically glance over at man who was less than two feet from his wife, with a silencer attached to a 9mm pointed at her head as she slept peacefully.

The weather continued to rumble. The downpour was steady and the thunder along with the lightning continued to shake up the outdoors.

Xavier's wife, Bria, had an undiagnosed case of sleep inertia. She could sleep through anything and rainy nights she seemed to get the best sleep. Xavier would become so angry that his tender kisses couldn't awake her. This was the one time he didn't find himself becoming upset about his wife's terrible sleeping habits. Bria slept as though she didn't have a care in the world. He prayed she wouldn't be awakened by the demands of the masked individual. He was only mad at himself for being the big brother

The Young and the Reckless

trying to help the little brother, allowing him to stash his illegal money in his modest home. The custom made safe depicted an overprice nightstand that he knew that his little brother had to be running his mouth about. He knew his brother like to boast and brag. It was a bad characteristic that he had possessed ever since they were little kids. He never imagined that his little brother's boasting, and bragging would lead him to this life or death moment.

    Xavier's vision became blurred as the liquid substance cascaded down his cheeks leaving a salty taste on his lips. He hadn't uttered another sound. Xavier said a silent prayer hoping that his wife would not wake up and become frightened by what was taken place in her sanctuary. The March winds were not alone on this night. The wind would tap on the window pane just loud enough to get the attention of anyone who was listening then whisk on to its next mission. The boom of the thunder could sporadically be heard. Then there was the two malicious men accompanied the rhythm of the pitter patter, wearing nothing but mayhem as though it was a tailored made suit.

    Before Xavier could respond, the piercing soft suppressed sound off the gunshot sent a ringing through his ears and a chill through his body that shook his soul. His tears stopped, and eyes became filled with rage. At that moment, Xavier didn't know whether to fight for his life or attempt to make a run for it. Just a few feet away in his bedroom closet was his protection for the house. He knew he wasn't able to get to it, even if he was given a head start. He'd have to open the case it was tucked away in. He wanted his children's life spared, but he knew he couldn't go on without Bria. For a split second, he was ready to join his wife. The thought of his children being in this cruel world without both parents was something he couldn't fathom. He looked at the guy that was standing over him. He noticed that he appeared just as devastated as he was from the other individual pulling the trigger. Suddenly his life flashed before his eyes. Quick as a wink he no longer cared about living.

The masked man which stood over his wife's lifeless body had loosened his grip on the gun just enough that Xavier fixated his eyes on the familiar image engraved on the handle of this black and army green Smith and Wesson 9mm. Before he could make the decision to decide if he should fight his way out or say a few more words to plead his case, his lifeless body slumped to the floor.

The sound of the phone ringing startled Cinque. Three days in a row he had dreamed about his parent's murder. It had been seven years and the crime had yet to be solved. He smiled as he watched Star's name and picture come across the screen of his phone. He smiled admiring her moisturized mocha complexion, "Hello." The birthmark that flowed from her hairline onto her forehead didn't intercede with her beauty. He always thought it made her quite unique. It was just the opposite for her. Star thought her birthmark that resembled the bottom portion of South Africa was

The Young and the Reckless

hideous and she always hid it with a baseball cap or bangs.

"Hey, Cinque this is Star. Well of course you know it is me, my name is programmed in your phone right," she blushed and felt a little lame. She continued with her reason for calling, "I hate to disappoint you, but I'm not having any good vibes about this little getaway. I was a slightly excited at first thinking about this road trip, but my gut feeling is telling me that this is not going to end well." Star took her time as she chose her words carefully. "I know you said we could shop. Lord knows I need some new clothes but." She thought about how often she chose a regular white cotton A-shirt, known mostly as a wife beater, to put on as her daily attire. She had plenty of them. She paused and took a deep breath, "I really can't explain it, but something does not sit right with me about this trip."

"Come on Star. You can't do this to me. You do not have to worry about anything. I am not going to put you in any type of compromising situation. I just figured we can catch up on old times and get to know one another all over again. I promise I will not try anything." Cinque moved his lips to the left as far as they could go. He was glad his phone had ranged and interrupted the nightmare that had haunted him ever since he was ten-years-old. He sat with his right pointer finger placed on his lips as he thought about how he was going to respond. He wanted some answers and he thought at least once he would see some sort of sign that would reveal the people who he sought to give the ultimate payback. If it was there, he hadn't noticed it in seven years, but he was not about to give up.

"Cinque, I am not worried about you trying anything. I've been bullying you since we were about four years old. Do you think things changed just because we're older now?" Star teased.

"Girl, a lot has changed. You seem to be a tad bit confused. Let me get you hip really quick. We not four and I'm on big boy status now. I don't get bullied. I am the bully. So, go ahead and get ready and I'll be there around six in the morning. And you can drop the Cin and just call me Que." Cinque let her know that they could talk face to face about this trip. He ended the call before Star could rebuttal.

Cinque looked at the time on his cell phone. He had twelve hours until it was time to hit the road. He packed an overnight bag, so Star would think they would be spending the night in Chicago. He had it all mapped out. He knew if they were on the road by seven, they would make it to their destination by twelve. His plan was to stop and get something to eat at the Frontera Grill, check in to the hotel, shop, pick up his package, rest for an hour, and get back on the road and head back home.

Cinque was making his way towards Star's house. He hadn't been on that side of the town since he was 10 years old. A lot had changed since he had left. Vacant buildings that were practically falling down outnumbered the occupied homes. Running into Star a few weeks back had brought him back to his roots. When he came back to the neighborhood

The Young and the Reckless

the first time to meet Star was the first night that the nightmares resurfaced. Now the last two weeks that gruesome image from the worse day of his life had a constant presence in his thoughts rerunning like old episodes of *Martin* on *BET*.

Cinque admired the leaves on the maple trees as he drove down the street. The leaves were turning from yellow to orange and soon to be red before the all became green. It was a perfect spring photo. As he was about to turn down his old street, he thought he was reliving a scene from his past. Red, blue and white lights were sporadically flashing and interrupted the scenery of spring he was admiring as he cruised his old neighborhood. Three police cars and an ambulance had the two-way street blocked off in both directions. He was curious to know what was going on this early in the morning. He parked his car not far from the corner, got out the car and made his way down the street.

Cinque saw a familiar face as headed toward Star's home. He noticed Star's mother just screaming and hollering. It was early in the morning and people were out parleying as if it were noon. Some individuals had on clothes like they were headed to work while others were draped in pajamas and housecoats. Cinque could see nothing had changed. Drama bought everyone on the block out the house winter, spring, summer and fall. He rushed over to Star's mother and she immediately grabbed him and held on tight. He hadn't been held in such a manner in quite some time. Tears rolled down his face from his eyes just from the current embrace that he had been longing for a while.

Together they stood there crying. Neither one of them knew why either of them were shedding tears. He wondered did she even know who he was. To his dismay, she knew exactly who he was.

    Cinque was a spitting image of his dad Xavier and his uncle Pharaoh who like to be referred as Hot Rod. Patty admired his rich caramel skin, the sternness in which their eyes seem to always have and the broad protruding nose that made them appear very serious at all times. He even had the precise lined deep black haircut that was neatly trimmed and never out of place. He had been by there lately, but he never ran into her. He honestly thought that she had run off because she had dreams of being a Hollywood star. She had a face for television.

    Star's mother hadn't uttered a simple word. He had the look of confusion on his face as he was trying to figure out what was going on. She had her head buried in his chest. With her being in his arms, he stepped back and looked at the crowd. As he stood near the front of the ambulance, he noticed that the paramedics had the back doors open to the ambulance. He could tell they were working on someone and he needed to know who, but his fears had taken over him. He kept scanning the crowd. His curiosity grew wanting to know who was in the ambulance. He began to take baby steps as he held on to Patty, easing them to the back of the ambulance. As he moved inch by inch, Cinque was surveying the crowd to see if he could see Star. As they reached the door of the ambulance, he had a sigh of relief. Star had surfaced from the ambulance.

The Young and the Reckless

Star hopped down off the back of the ambulance and headed over to Cinque and shook her head. "Ma, are you going to ride in the ambulance with Nanna?" Star stood there waiting on her mother's response with the ugliest attitude.

Cinque was so glad to see her. Just seeing her gave him a sense of relief. He let go of Star's mother and began to embrace Star. He looked up to the sky, "Thank you!" he whispered.

Star looked at Cinque strangely and chuckled, "Boy, what's wrong with you? And I know you didn't just thank God!?" Star was referring to a conversation they had previously when he stated he and God were not on the best of terms and hadn't been in years.

"I actually thought something had happened to you. When I saw your mother standing here all alone crying. I got nervous. I damn near panicked. You hear me." Cinque chortled.

"As you can see, nothing has happened to me. My grandmother fell and bumped her head. She claimed she lost balance as she was getting out of her bed. I noticed the blood at the top of her head and called 911. Patty out here doing too much and the paramedics had to call for backup. They just let her out of the police car!" Star looked at her mother with disgust. Star had been acting more like the mother lately.

"I see she hasn't changed. Always got to be dramatic." Cinque looked over in Patty's direction.

"We'll Cinque, I am not going to be able to take this road trip. So, you can go ahead, I'm about to go to this hospital with my Nanna and make sure everything's okay with her." Star sighed to Cinque.

"Que! How many times do I have to tell you that?" He declared, "Let me make this phone call and I can follow you all to the hospital." Cinque kissed Star on her forehead and walked back to his car. He had to walk pass his childhood home to make it to his car. He avoided looking in the direction of the home. He blocked the house out. In his mind he had removed from the street. To him it was a vacant lot were the house remained.

The police cleared the traffic and the onlookers started to disperse. Cinque picked up the phone and called his little sister as he got in his car so that he could be ready to pull off behind the ambulance. The ambulance drove through the city streets in silence with the sirens on mute only flashing their lights. Cinque followed behind the ambulance with a steady pace and distance.

Cinque let the phone ring several of times. He had to dial her back once her voicemail came on. When he noticed she answered the phone, he began to speak, "Nevaeh, listen." He instructed, "I need you to do me a huge favor and you cannot say, no."

The Young and the Reckless

Nevaeh rolled her eyes, "I should have known you wanted something call me this early. What is it now?"

"Look I'm about to head to this hospital with Star. I don't know how long I am going to be up here, and I got to be at that place for Unc. You know that little thing you did before for me when I threw that kickback and couldn't go myself." He didn't wait for her to answer, "I need you to do it again. One more time for the one time, please."

"That's all? I thought you wanted something major. Like, be Carlos girlfriend again. I'm game. But, let me tell you this now, it is going to cost you more. What time you want me to leave?"

Cinque paused. He wasn't worried about the price. He was going to pay it regardless. He was kind of hesitant about how urgent he needed this to be done and how she would reply. He didn't know how she was going to respond when he said right now.

"Hello. Did you hear me, boy?" Nevaeh grew a tad bit frustrated.

Cinque was hesitant, but he spoke softly, "Right now,"

"Right now! You got to be kidding me. You don't' know what I had planned for the day. I am still celebrating my birthday. This is really going to cost you more. Last minute. I don't even know if I could get someone to ride with me on such a short notice." Nevaeh shook her head. She would never tell her big brother no and she knew he would never tell her no either.

"Call Paradise." Cinque smiled waiting on Nevaeh to respond.

"Yeah, I will call her, and you bet not ignore her call when she calls you." Nevaeh wanted to give him a hard time, but she was hesitant. She murmured, "Que, I'm about to call Paradise. One!" Nevaeh pressed end.

Before she could get to Paradise's name in her phone, Big Bro came across her screen. She started to press ignore send him so the voicemail, but she knew he called right back.

"What now?" Nevaeh waited on what he had to say.

"Dude expecting you at four. So look here, call me when you are getting on the highway, call me as soon as you get to Bloomington, Illinois call me as soon as you get off I-55, call me when you pull up to the spot, call me when you leave the spot, call me when you are getting back on I-55, Call me again when you reach Bloomington. Do the speed limit and use your signals every time you switch lanes". Got that?"

Nevaeh interrupted, "Dude I know. Same as before. One!"

The Young and the Reckless

He hated when she said that. Ever since she seen the movie *Belly* and DMX would say it when he hung up the phone, she thought that was just the greatest thing. She said that was better than saying the word bye. One day she told him bye meant gone forever and she hated the thought of forever.

Paradise had agreed. She was Neveah's only choice and only friend. Nevaeh had picked up Paradise hit the highway and made her phone calls as instructed. When she made her last phone call, it would be the phone call that Cinque did not want to hear nor was he expecting it. Nevaeh looked in the rearview mirror and watched the flashing lights as she placed her call to her brother.

"Hey Que, I just want you to know, we just got pulled over. The cop just took my license I walked back to his car. So now we just sitting here waiting." She looked in the rearview watching the officer, "I should pull off on his ass."

"Where you gonna go when you pull off? Anyway. Did you do the speed limit and use your signals like I told you?" He spoke calm and firm.

"They not applying no pressure right now. The cop pulled me over and said the police are looking for a black Ford Escape that wanted for questioning in some shooting."

Que was pissed at this point, "They say anything to justify stupid shit. I guess they were looking for Missouri plates, too?"

"Right. I should have asked did the car have Missouri plates. You know I haven't shot anyone. I should be cool, but I will call you back in a second." Nevaeh pressed end and deleted her incoming and outgoing call log.

Paradise looked in her rearview, "Damn. Four more cars just pulled up just for us. If we have to go to the station don't be on that rah-rah mess. I ain't ready to be taken to the King." Paradise gasped.

Nevaeh and Paradise both looked in their rearview mirrors. They sat in silence as they watched more police cruisers pull up to the scene.

The Young and the Reckless

CHAPTER 2

The treble and the bass began to synch to the heartbeat of everyone that could hear the music. The upbeat rhythm and tone had the patron's mood feeling harmonious. The DJ was playing everything from Drake, Future, Lil Uzi Vert and Kendrick Lamar. The conversations of the partygoers were constantly being drown out. A few danced while others watched the dancers do their thing. The DJ announced each dancer as they made their way to the stage. A few dancers stripped teased while others did acrobatic types of tricks on the burlesque pole. The dancers were not discreet as the detained those determined to spend dollars during the duration of the hustle and bustle of the club. Not a single nipple was covered by pasties. There was no money unattended nor no table dance refused. Every dancer was topless. There was only a few walking around in their birthday suits. Every once in a while, someone would chant D Savage referring to Demond's rapper name. The DJ had even given him a few shout outs.

Cinque and Kavon were enjoying being able to ride the wave of Demond being a local celebrity. Just about everywhere they went they were treated like hood royalty. Tonight, was no different. Demond had placed a few of his rap videos on YouTube and was receiving the views that made him a well-known artist. Demond was the sole reason people flocked to surround them. The three of them sat at the round table which was in the front center of the stage in Bottom's Up strip club enjoying their lap dances from the females who were looking for the men who spent the most dollars.

Bottom's Up is best known for their exotic dancers. It's like Atlanta's Magic City or King of Diamonds but located in Collinsville, Illinois right outside of East St. Louis. It became the most frequent spot once the Pink Slip closed which was right up the street. The Pink Slip had every shape and size you could think of working in that establishment. Bottom's Up was a little bit more selective of the women who worked there.

A few individuals that the boys knew were there with them amongst the crowd. They didn't ride together but the met up there. The females and the fellas were all surrounded by them Snap Chatting and Instagramming. Money was been thrown and spent. Kavon noticed that a crowd of raunchy, yet grimy individuals were not enjoying the club scene as much as he and his crew. He leaned in to let Que know and he let him know he had already peeped it. Kavon tapped Demond and leaned in to whisper in his ear, "We gotta bounce."

Although the music was loud, Demond heard exactly what he whispered. The weary look Kavon had in his eyes let Demond know it would be in his best interest to follow him to the exit door and not waste any time. Demond was enjoying his star status attention and wasn't really ready to leave.

The Young and the Reckless

People were sending him drinks and asking for photos. The attention may have been overwhelming for some but not for him. Majority of the time it was Cinque in the spotlight but not today. He knew leaving as his friend instructed would be in his best interest.

The three of them exited the club swiftly and made it to Que's car without any problems. As soon as they crossed the bridge into St. Louis and was about to make the right turn to merge onto the interstate that would lead them home, the flashing lights brought them to a pause.

"Everyone out of the car!" the officer demanded. He spoke loud enough he could be heard through the raised window. They all followed the orders with no hesitation, nor questions and exited the car with their hands up in the air in the don't shoot position. The officers were unaware that they had pulled over a local hood celebrity. He didn't care about them being hood royalty and spoke to them as though they were yesterday's trash.

One officer positioned himself near the back of the car on the passenger side with his hand laying on his service revolver, ready to pull it out as if he were in a standoff in the Wild Wild West. The first officer who initially told them to exit the vehicle instructed them all to stand on the passenger side of the car. Kavon was the first to be slammed down to the hood of the car then handcuffed. After the handcuffs were placed on him, the officer helped him down to the sitting position on the curb. Demond and Cinque still with their hands up watched and awaited who would be next. Demond was handled roughly next sustaining the same procedure as Kavon. He turned and told Cinque to sit down on next to his homeboys. The officer figured Cinque was most likely be the one to run because he was the driver of the vehicle.

Each one of them were fueled with anger and fear. Angry because they were being treated as though they were unworthy humans. While fearing to become the next hashtag had them shook. Neither of them asked any questions of why they were pulled over. Trying yet to understand why they hadn't been asked about a license or registration. No one said anything but were all having similar thoughts. Together without saying one word they didn't want either officer to fear for their life as they were doing at that moment. They just wanted to make it home alive and in one piece. It was four in the morning and no one was out to even witness the injustice that was occurring. A few cars passed by but all of them just rolled by. The second officer walked up and began to search the car.

Cinque became awfully nervous. He placed his right finger over his lips and rested his chin on his thumb. His stashbox was behind his radio. His uncle had it installed for him. It was one button on the radio screen that you pushed to reveal his Glock. Just as the other officer went to assist in the illegal search, a call came over the radio. An officer had been shot and apparently it was more important than harassing three young black men who had just had a few drinks and flossed a few dollars in a strip club. Kavon and Demond were released from the

The Young and the Reckless

handcuffs by the officer who placed them on the two of them.

Cinque drove them all to his home. The entire ride was a silent one. The thoughts that ran through their minds were images of all the black individuals who were gunned down by white officers who received paid leave when they committed murders.

Grateful they made it to their destination in one piece, they called it a night. They had known idea the next day would be just eventful.

"Latrell is straight wilding out. He just posted on the *Book*, who got gas and mobile? Then some dude name J-Rock told him to drop his location and he did it." Demond stood up and walked over to the barber chair where Que was getting his hair trimmed by Kavon. He put his cellular device in Que's face, so he could see the status himself. Sure, enough Latrell had dropped his location.

Kavon looked down into the phone with his glasses on the tip of his nose and a toothpick protruding from his mouth. He read the status along with Que. He put his clippers down when he saw what he needed to see. He spun the chair around. He and Que were now face to face. Looking directly in Que's eyes he spoke with authority, "We need to go handle that. We need to go give this weak dude the blues. He needs to be taught the do's and don'ts of this game."

"Say less." Que stood up and removed the black plastic barber cape. He was just getting touched up. He really didn't need a fresh cut. Having a day one he who had mad skills when it came to the clippers, he never walked around without a fresh cut. He and his two friends were in his uncle's home in the basement of the makeshift barbershop. Kavon didn't have a license to barber, he just possessed the gift of one who had a license. He had become everyone's barber but right now he was about to use another one of his many talents.

Que and his friends made their way out of his uncle's home he and his sister had been living in since the death of their parents. It was Uncle Pharaoh or his grandparents. His grandparents had moved away from civilization. That's how Cinque felt when they would drive to visit his grandparents. He convinced Nevaeh they needed to stay with their cool uncle who always dropped cash on them whenever he graced them with his presence. Pharaoh didn't have to be asked. He just gave.

Their residence was tucked away on a cul-de-sac in a quiet community just thirty-minutes from the block they called their set. They trapped from one of the properties his grandparents owned. It was the home where Xavier and Pharaoh grew up. His grandmother was unaware of what was taken place where she once resided. She and her husband trusted Pharaoh to take care of their old properties. After the death of their son Xavier they had moved away from the city of St. Louis and had taken up a new residence that was nearly two hours away. Que knew his father wouldn't be proud of what he was doing. Que felt the presence of his father every time he stepped foot in the three-bedroom house. He

The Young and the Reckless

didn't want to be anywhere else because he could feel his dad's presence.

Que slowly drove down the street two blocks from his home. Kavon hopped out with tool in hand. In less than forty-five seconds Kavon had found the vehicle and began to trail Que to the set. Que headed towards his family's old home with Demond in tow. Once Que parked, he and Demond exited the vehicle. Que had his door key in hand, opened the door, entered the four-digit code in the alarm's key pad. Kavon dimmed the lights as he sat in the car waiting on them to come back out.

Que walked towards the back of the house to go to basement of the home. The home was unoccupied, and it showed. The kitchen looked different from the rest of the house. Only one of the three bedrooms were occupied with a mattress and box spring which was on the floor. The living room had an old beat up burgundy velvet couch. The kitchen could be compared to vvs diamonds. The kitchen looked fresh off of a showroom floor. Black cabinets, chrome finishes and stainless-steel appliances made the kitchen look very sleek. The white granite counters matched the table set perfectly. The kitchen and bathroom were updated in the event the Pharaoh needed to sell the property.

Que and Demond made it to the basement of the house. Que took a few steps and reached out to fumble for the light switch. Once the lights were on, they both proceeded to the area they came for. Que then walked over to the reason he was there and opened the stainless-steel gun cabinet. To the average person the stainless-steel cabinet looked like a 48-inch Whirlpool refrigerator. Once it was opened the appearance was totally different. The artillery in the cabinet was an amenity of someone ready for a war would love and admire. Pharaoh had a love for guns and it showed. His inventory surpassed that of an area police department. Pharaoh didn't mind sharing his love with his nephew and close friends. Everyone knew they had their own personal gun shop due to Pharaoh. His gun collection was the reason many called him Hot Rod. Cinque handed the AK-47 with a 75-round drum to Demond. Then he grabbed two black 9mm Glocks and four 33 round magazines. Cinque and Demond made their way back to the vehicle Kavon was waiting for them in.

Kavon drove them to their destination looking like Mc Eight in the movie *Menace II Society* when he drove Cain and O-Dogg on their mission to retaliate on the dudes who had shot Cain and killed his cousin. Kavon got them to where they were going and let them out of the car. For about three minutes it sounded like an atomic blast as rounds were being fired on the battle ground of the streets. Latrell was running for his life without a minute to spare. With guns hot and smoking Cinque and Demond hoped back into the box and Kavon skirted off.

Que felt his phone vibrating. He looked down and seen it was Star and he immediately answered. He had been waiting on her to call ever since he bust that u-ie when he seen her standing outside the church talking amongst a few females around the

The Young and the Reckless

corner from where he put in his work on daily. It had been seven years and she had not changed a bit in the face area. Her body had blossomed. Her curves could be seen in the hunter green maxi dress she was wearing on the day they reconnected. She was still hiding that bold black birthmark on her forehead. The sun was beaming down playing security toward the smooth spring breeze.

The church was having a youth explosion event. He had seen the flyer and church members had been canvassing the neighborhood for a week or so passing out the literature for the youth explosion. They were handing out literature that spoke about their belief that the youth was the future and should be involved with Christ just as much as adults. Apparently, it was going to be a huge event. Que stared at the flyer that stated the phrase, "train up a child in the way he should go and when he is old, he will not depart from it." He was at church quite frequently for the first ten years of his life. His mother sang in a choir and was a member of the usher board when she wasn't singing. Church was in her DNA. Her father was a Pastor of a mega church in Nashville, Tennessee. Her mother was the daughter of Pastor. Cinque's dad attended regularly as well but he wasn't an active member, nor did he come from a family of embedded church members or goers.

Que hadn't seen an inside of a church since his parent's double funeral. He had placed the literature in his pocket. He held on to it, he hadn't thrown it away, but he had no plans on attending. He was just glad that the event had taken place because it brought his longtime friend back into his life. As he drove by the church on the youth explosion day, he saw an image that caught his eye and he was very pleased. Que double-parked and walked right up to the crowd that was occupying Star's attention.

"I see you haven't embraced that beauty mark in all these years." He said with the biggest smile.

Star turned as though she had seen a ghost. She embraced his neck and her eyes began to water. She stepped back to check him out. She grabbed his hand and walked him away from her two friends Nadia & Davida. She felt this conversation was going to need some privacy. Star looked toward the street and seen the female that was watching them like a hawk about to demolish its prey sitting in the double-parked car.

"Cinque, it has been a long time. How have you been?" Star babbled as she waited for his response.

Cinque couldn't help to notice how Serenity was watching his every move, but he couldn't let this opportunity pass him by. He didn't know if he would see Star again. He didn't even think about visiting the old neighborhood to see if she still stayed that way. Deep down inside he didn't really want to go that way because of the memory he tried so hard to bury but couldn't. A car began to blow, and he felt that he was saved by the horn. He already had the encounter figured out. He was going to tell Serenity

The Young and the Reckless

that Star was his cousin he hadn't seen in a long time on his mother side of the family.

"Hey, let me get your number so we can catch up." He asked.

She raised her cell phone she already had in her hand, "What's your number?"

He gave her his number. She dialed it immediately. He looked down at his phone as he held it in his hand and recited the number back to her ensuring it was her that was calling. He back peddled away letting her know he would call her later. He then turned and trotted away from the church to back in the car. He couldn't look Serenity in her face as he told the bold face lie about Star being his cousin on his mother side. It didn't make a difference how they were related. Cinque hadn't introduced Serenity to anyone other than Demond and Kavon. She seen his other friend Carlos a few occasions, but he wasn't around often.

Even though he told Serenity that Star was his cousin, she still deleted the number right out of his phone the first chance she had. He could only remember the first three numbers after the area code. He couldn't remember the last four. He wanted to say something about it to Serenity, but he decided against it. He placed a code on his phone and he knew that would keep her from getting in his phone in the future. When he seen the number again, he smiled. It took Star two weeks to call him.

Him saying, hello broke the silence that was in the black charger Kavon was driving back to the set.

"Hey, Star. I thought you were never going to call me."

"Actually, you said you were going to call me." Star rebuked.

"I know but you wouldn't believe what happened. I was trying to save your number and I deleted it by accident." Cinque recounted.

"Hold on," Star paused and let out a sigh.

"What are you doing?" Cinque asked as he could hear the sadness in Star's voice.

"I'm watching the news. This dude I went to school with was just murdered outside his grandmother's home. He was pronounced dead at the scene, but two other victims are in stable condition." Star looked intensely at the television. She said a small prayer as the reporter reported the story.

"These goofy ass dudes let these rap niggas soup them up. They think they can run off on the plug and ain't shit going to happen to them." Que said as he Demond and Kavon walked into the house they had just left in less than an hour ago.

Kavon and Demond looked at Que. Kavon asked, "Who are you on the phone with right now?"

"This Star." He knew the question was out of concern for the statement he just made. "She is

The Young and the Reckless

watching the news, and someone just got murked." Cinque smirked as if he was unaware of the murdered, she was speaking about.

Star continued, "This witness talking about how loud the gunfire sounded. He doesn't think the two that were rushed to the hospital will make it. I knew something was bound to happen to Latrell. I heard he has backdoored three of his homeboys. Then his stray bullet was responsible for the death of that nine-year-old girl who was sitting in the kitchen doing her homework in Dellwood, and plus I heard he killed someone's grandmother during a home invasion all because her grandson did something like smack one of his girl cousins."

Everything Star had mentioned about Latrell was true. He was young and reckless. He didn't care about his life or no one else. He had caused so much havoc and chaos in the streets of St. Louis. The police had his name in so much paperwork but there was no one to identify him. The police act as though it was hearsay. Latrell was the oldest of thirteen children and he was simply out in the world running amuck. His look was very deceiving. Latrell was five feet tall and resembled a young Terrance Howard. Nothing from his appearance said he was a malicious criminal. He lost his life just like his father did. In these streets love is weird. Love will get you killed and being killed gets you loved.

Que didn't really want to talk about what she was talking about. He let her know he was locking her number in and he was going to call her once he made it home. He quickly ended the call. He didn't want to come across as heartless to Star.

"We need to hurry up and get rid of that box!" Kavon said referring to the car he a just stole. "I know they are probably out here looking for it."

They put the weapons that they had just used back up in the stainless-steel gun cabinet as though they had never removed them. Leaving the same way, they came they were in and out the house. A few guys from their crew was standing outside hugging the block. The boys acknowledge their presence but kept it moving. Kavon paid close attention to who was all standing on the block posted like a lamppost. He made a mental note in case he had to pay a few people a visit for running off at the mouth. The block huggers observed them dressed in all black. They weren't sure of what happened, but they could make speculations just from the attire and the weapons they had seen them exit with from the vehicle.

The unknown car they were in when they pulled up in was a dead giveaway that something had just went down. No one really cared about seeing one another because the streets have a code, and many will die by that code. Street justice is what many refer to it as. Kavon, Que and Demond just gained major respect from the block huggers. The unspoken code had unearned them some respect and although people may make mention of what they saw or witness someone will handle it to make sure they wouldn't speak of it. And the few that were out there knew the code wasn't worth breaking. Cinque was the reasoning many of them were able to feed their family and no one is going to bite the

The Young and the Reckless

hand that feeds them. One might think he was lucky to be amongst this type of loyalty.

    Kavon drove the car trying to find the perfect location to leave it. He was trying to avoid any and all cameras by any means necessary. He found the perfect location. Kavon parked and exited the vehicle. He pulled off his gloves and placed them in his back pocket. He hopped in the car with Que and Demond.

CHAPTER 3

The serene night had slowly faded away as the morning gradually made its debut. The words to the songs of cars occasionally driving by playing loud music could barely be heard. This remoteness of the sound seemed far but they were right outside the window of the busy city street Serenity lived on. The sounds of a few chirping birds could be heard in the distance. The smoke detector's chirp was in competition with the few birds who were a few feet away outside of the window. The constant beeping was slightly annoying, but no one had been in a rush to change the battery although it was long overdue.

Serenity rested in her twin size bed with very severe stomach cramps. She was feeling as though the soldiers in Afghanistan were all tap dancing on her bladder trying to get home to freedom. Serenity had just about enough. She was trying to get just a little more sleep, but she couldn't take it anymore. Serenity finally decided to get up and pay her own personal water bill. Right as she was about to enter the bathroom, she could hear what she thought was her mother and her new man she currently was dating about to enter their home. Serenity didn't

The Young and the Reckless

understand why her mother was now seeing her once close friend's ex. Mr. Sloppy seconds was keeping her mother away from home what Serenity felt was too much time away from her children. However, she felt she could hold it down until her mother remembered her responsibilities. Serenity believed they knew what they were doing was wrong and her mother didn't want to get caught with him in her home by none of their other friends. Nevertheless, she was glad that her mother had finally made it home. The knock at the front door seemed to have startled Serenity. She jumped nearly wetting her black and white *PINK* boy shorts. Serenity realized it was someone at the front door that apparently, they didn't have a key.

As she was about to go assist them since they appeared to be having a difficult time getting in the house, she quickly changed her mind. Serenity was taken notice to the annihilation Vicki had been performing to her mother's vehicle on a weekly basis since she and Jackson became more than just friends. Vicki had bust the window and Jackson had it fixed. She'd come bust two more windows. Vicki would flatten the tire a he'd get that fix. Then she would come back and flatten two more tires. For the last month Serenity mom's car has been looking like an abandon vehicle in front of their home. All four tires were flat, no windows to this '09 hard top once turquoise Mustang. It was so much graffiti on this car from phrases like MAN STEALER, BITCH, HE IS MINE, WHORE, HOME WRECKER, and GET YOUR OWN MAN. This car had just as much words on it as the Webster's dictionary had in it.

BOOM! Was the next sound Serenity had heard coming from the main entrance of her home. It was as though a B-100, armored vehicle was trying to invade her space. The loud boom made her snap out of her thoughts and forget all about her need to release her bladder. Now she knew this couldn't be her mother's friend Vicki because she wasn't screaming Mona along with other obscenities. Vicki had never tried to make an entrance into their home before, so she knew this couldn't be her. Her motive could have changed. There was nothing left to do to the car but set it on fire. Jackson stopped getting the repairs done when all Vicki would do was come right back and destroy it again. She would come like a thief in the night when she did damage to the vehicle. Vicki went unheard but not unseen. Serenity knew this erratic behavior was different. Vicki had never tried to harm Mona's or her children before. Serenity was trying to figure out who was trying to enter her home. Whomever was on the other side of the door had some sense of urgency to get in their home. When she seen the light creeping through the crack as the front door was slowly given in, she suddenly realized that this was someone on the other side of the door was trying to forcefully enter their home. Serenity ran and dove into her bed.

The blackness of the night was gradually fading away as the sun was slowly creeping on the

The Young and the Reckless

horizon. Serenity didn't have to run far because her bed was in the room right off the living room, which made her bed diagonal from the front door and she could see the door bend as it was being kicked. Then she realized her brother was all alone in her mother's bedroom. She headed towards her brother. The distance from her mother's room from her bed only took approximately twelve steps. Serenity peaked around the corner from the bedroom looked at the door and seen they hadn't made it in the house. The deadbolt lock was slowing down their process. She crept swiftly and softly to her mother's room. She looked back to make sure they didn't see any movement she was making. The noise of the banging stopped, and she let out a sigh of relief. Serenity climbed right in the king-sized bed with her brother. As soon as he was in the bed the noise from the intruders trying to gain entrance into the home continued.

  Cameron was out for the count. Football practice had worn him out. She was so surprised that the almost intruders couldn't hear him snoring. Football practice was Tuesday, Thursday, and Friday. Friday was the day before game day and they practiced harder than ever before the game. The Junior Football League who he played for made sure the teams were ready for their Saturday or Sunday games. The practice field was in walking distance from their home. She made sure that he made it there every day scheduled. They didn't have problems with the neighborhood scoundrels because her mother, Mona, grew up in the very same neighborhood. Everyone knew she didn't play about her kids. Everyone thought she was two sandwiches short of the picnic anyway. Mona was a fighter when she was coming up. She always had to defend herself because she looked so different from everyone else in the neighborhood. Right now, Vicki was the only one that could care less about the reputation Serenity's mother had. Mona slept in the very same room which Cameron and Serenity shared. Her mother, Serenity's grandmother, left Mona the house when she went to Indonesia to teach English. One year turned to eight and Grandma Monica had been gone just as long as Cameron and Serenity's dad.

    Right now, Serenity wished she was in Indonesia with her grandmother because who ever had just made it in the house was not invited. She had no clue to why someone was trying to enter her home. She hated that the backdoor was barricaded by the refrigerator on one side and trash on the other side. The backdoor was to keep people from doing what the unknown individuals were doing at the front door.

    Serenity could hear whispers and loud footsteps coming closer to her mother's room. Things were being shoved and tossed. They had just couldn't kicked the door in to get in the home. It took some time and effort, but they had made it in and apparently the nosey neighbors weren't being so nosey. They were being loud enough for Serenity

The Young and the Reckless

to hear but not loud enough for any neighbors to be concerned. She was so surprised that her brother didn't budge, but practice had done him in a few hours earlier. He was too tired to eat. Cameron turned Que down to grab something to eat before he had dropped them off at home.

She was quite sure her neighbor Ms. Tina, who sees and hears everything on the block must have been gone on her rendezvous to the Ameristar Casino. Ms. Tina would have been called the police when she seen them walk up on the porch. Ms. Tina lived across the street and she was the current captain of the block of neighborhood watch. She knew the comings and goings of just about everybody in her porch's view vicinity. In Young Jeezy's song J.E.E.Z.Y, when he says the old lady across the street still bitching, at three in the morning he was telling her take her old ass to sleep because it was the third time, she had called the police in a week. He had to been speaking about Ms. Tina. She'd use binoculars Serenity ordered for her off eBay to get closer viewings of what she couldn't see from her front porch. She should have been getting a hearing aid because she couldn't hear to save her life. Ms. Tina is the boys in blue groupie. She did her stint in the political arena in her early years. She and Serenity's grandmother were good friends with the grandmother of the city's current police chief, Steven Styles.

Serenity pinched herself to make sure she wasn't in a bad dream. Instantly her body went numb. Frightening by fear and suddenly becoming faintheartedness had her paralyzed. She couldn't tell if she had pinched herself or not. Just when she thought about the intruders, she thought it could possibly be her mother Mona trying to get in their home. Maybe Mona was about to surprise them. They were supposed to go shopping and out to eat. Mona hated breaking the promises she made to her children, so she may just have a sense of urgency to get in the home and possibly misplaced her door keys. Jackson came into her life giving her the attention she had be longing for and Mona had forgot all about her responsibilities. She was thinking that maybe Mona had come to her senses and realized she was making a major mistake. For the past three months she was apparently living her best life kid free. She had been tearing down the malls and going on shopping sprees. Serenity felt as though her mother was trying to resurface and do the things she did before Jackson entered the picture. Serenity began to shiver wishing that it was her mother and she had forgotten her key again.

All Serenity could see was the pearly whites of this unknown man eyes who was standing in Mona's bedroom. Serenity felt violated. The glare coming from the window of the sunlight didn't help any. It was only bright enough to see that this individual was dressed in all black wearing a black ski mask. When the ski masked man turned and stood over Cameron and Serenity, she felt the worst was about to happen. He turned and walked out the

The Young and the Reckless

room. She gave a little peak, but she remained calm, still and quiet just before the worst storm was about to hit.

Just as she thought it was safe to grab the phone and dial 911 there now stood three individuals in all black. Her grandmother always said that Cameron sounded just like grandpa when he snored. "Cameron, in there calling those hogs!" she would scream. He was calling somebody but the only people there to answer were Serenity and the men in black. Neither one of them did anything.

She gently closed her eyes and held her breath. She wanted to fake snore, but she felt as though someone held their hand around my mouth and the snore wouldn't come out. Whatever and whomever kept her quiet should have done the same for Cameron. He let out a thundering car crash sound and startled everyone in the room. Serenity was the only one that didn't jump. For one she was used to it and two the men in black would have known she was not asleep.

Serenity rested in the bed under the leopard print comforter with her back towards her brother. She was positioned under the cover where she could peek without being seen. She had the cover just enough to peek from under it to see what was going on. She fought desperately not to turn and look back at Cameron. She felt the men in black in the bedroom and they had to be standing alongside her brother. They were not in her view. She felt their presence in the room but when opened her eyes a little to peek, she didn't see a soul. One of them began to open her mother's closet door. Then one on of the individuals spoke in a low southern drawl, "Silly mu-fucka! Do you see that?"

"Whaaat?" the other dude spoke in a high pitch tone displaying his pearly white teeth. You would have thought Chris Tucker was in the room from the way he sounded.

The southern individual answered, "These damn kids. I thought they left every Friday with that freak, Mona!"

"Man, they always do but they sleep. We can just get this safe and we out!" the knock-off Chris Tucker responded.

"Dude, what if these damn kids wake up and we all up in here trying to get their daddy's safe?" he slowly spoke in his southern drawl.

"Watch out for that lil nigga! I hear he a beast. He gotta strong lil tackle on'em." The knock off Chris Tucker warned them. He turned to the third individual who hadn't said a word, "Dude, what's up? What's taking so long? You ain't found that safe yet? This damn house ain't that damn big. The living room, the kid's room, Mona room, kitchen, bathroom and basement."

The quiet individual didn't say a word he just shook his head and moved the flashlight around the

The Young and the Reckless

closet. He began showing him and nothing was there.

Things almost turned for the worst as she felt this individual rubbing her hair. Serenity's hair was soft with thick black natural deep waves. Women spent money on her type of hair. Some say its good hair, but it wasn't good to her. She couldn't do anything with it. If she wore it straight it would draw up from the humidity. So, a ponytail was her only friend. She usually slept with it brushed up in her everyday ponytail. She had washed it when she made it home and now it was all over her head. She knew it was going to be tangled, but it didn't matter. All she was going to do was brush it up in her usually ponytail and let the fuzz hang. If she were going anywhere special, she would place it in a bun.

"You should have been my daughter but yo momma loved that nigga C-Note dirty drawls. See I would still be out here to tame that little freak. She out here running these streets like some hoe with no direction." As this southerner spoke, Serenity now knew that their house wasn't just a random break in. Her cover was about to be blown had he stroke her hair one more time. Serenity felt the warmness of the liquid leaving her body. Right as he made his last stroke, he ran his finger down her back and placed his hand her my derriere. Had he gone any further down he would have felt her wetness that he caused. He was distracted by the scream of the knock off Chris Tucker.

"Damn man," he said, "Fuck it! Go in there and see if they have some trash bags. We can take this bitch shit. We can sale this shit and get a few dollars. She still got shit with tags on it. I know we can get a few dollars. Her crazy ass boosted this shit anyway."

The one guy that hadn't said a word left and came right back with the trash bags.

Then the other one continued with his high pitch, "Yeah, we can go sell some this shit to Vicki, so Mona will think she had something to do with her door being off the hinges."

The southerner walked away from Serenity towards Mona's dresser. He went right for the jewelry box. The individual that hadn't said a word joined him. As the moon was disappearing and the sun was slowly making its presence the light reflected on his left hand and she could see a red cardinal bird tatted on his hand between his thumb and pointer finger. Now she was able to identify all three of them. A southern drawl that reminded her of a dude Mona dated from Memphis, Chris Tucker's high pitch comedic voice and red Cardinal bird were some distinguished details to her. She made a mental note. She didn't know who she was going to tell because in eighteen days her dad would be a free man. After long eight years in prison she didn't want him to go right back. She thought about telling Jackson since he was acting like he was so in love with Mona. He had left his own readymade family to

The Young and the Reckless

come over there with Mona and her kids. Well not so much the kids because they were rarely there but he was always with Mona. Mona kept telling him he was going to have to leave because Carl was on his way home. Jackson didn't care, and he was spending all the time he could with Mona.

The intruders were gone, and things were now quiet. Cameron rose up. He looked at Serenity and she looked back at him. It was like looking in the mirror seeing both their dark mahogany skin tone and deep wavy black hair. Although they looked damn near the same, their features were distinctive enough to tell which one the boy was. Their dad couldn't deny them. They looked identical to him. It was just his skin tone was a smooth color of dark brown soil.

Mona was the reason their hair was the way it was. She got it from her dad whom she never knew. All she knew about him was his name was Akram. Akram is Arabic for most generous. The only thing he was generous with was his sperm and money. Serenity believed her grandmother, Monica, was really in love with him. From Serenity's own speculation, she concluded that Akram's mother wasn't fond of interracial dating. Akram's mother had never met Mona. Speaking of Mona, she had just come in the door as Cameron stood up. Cameron was trying to figure out why he was wet. He knew he hadn't peed himself.

Cameron looked down at Serenity. As he began to speak, he had a look of disgust on his face from the wetness on his jogging pant, "I thought you were going to give us up. I felt you just a moving. I am so surprised they didn't catch you moving." Cameron exclaimed.

She looked at him with a look of confusion because she just knew he was asleep. Then she mustered up some words, "You were faking sleep that entire time?"

He replied, "Yeah, Gustavo told me that some people broke in his house a week ago. He and his mother just laid there."

"Gustavo, your Mexican friend?" she nervously asked.

"Candace, how many Gustavo's do I know?" Cameron spoke in a very sarcastic tone.

"I know his dad is the head of some type of Mexican Mafia Cartel group or whatever and I am just surprised these fellows not dead by now. You know I watch the news every night. I haven't seen the headlines robbers brutally murdered." Serenity shot back.

Cameron began to undress. He ignored his sister although he chuckled to himself about the lie, he told her about Gustavo's dad being a part of a cartel. He just had a roofing business and they had built a nice little empire going in the roofing business.

The Young and the Reckless

His boxers were dry, but his pant was a little tainted. He was showing no fear. His reaction was as though this was something, he experienced all the time. The truth of the matter was that he had heard of so many home invasions from his classmates and players on his football team, he was just waiting on his turn. He had already mentally prepared himself.

Serenity on the other hand was terrified. She began to think about Que telling her about the time his parents were murdered doing a home invasion. The story sent chills through her as he gave her detail per detail of two masked men killing his mom and dad. She was even looking for an army green gun with a lion engraved on it. She thanked God her life had been spared. She could hear that her mother was finally home, but she was headed to the bathroom to clean herself up.

Serenity took one of those white boys showers her dad had told her about. She rinsed and slid into her mom's red robe that was on the back of the door. She could hear her mother speaking but couldn't make out the words. When she heard the slurred speech, she knew she had to be on her little blue pill. She came out the bathroom. Serenity and Cameron and began to walk towards their mother in the living room. Serenity made eye contact with Jackson as he stood over her mother while she sat on the black leather sofa. He looked at Serenity with a look of it wasn't me because of the look she was giving him, she knew Jackson had to know that she didn't care too much about him. The look of disgust was shown on Serenity's face as she turned her lip up towards Jackson as she gave him direct eye contact. Serenity had every intention of demeaning him as he sat with his stupid it wasn't me face expression.

Slowly Mona began to speak and enunciating every syllable, yet it was slurred, "What the fuck y'all being doing? Why is my front door laying in the middle of my mother fucking living room?"

Cameron and Serenity looked at each other as if to say which one of us going to answer her dumb ass.

Serenity looked at her and Cameron walked over to grab her. Serenity finally spoke, "I don't do hard questions!" As she walked to the phone Ms. Tina came running through where the door once stood.

Serenity couldn't understand why Jackson hadn't murmured a word. Why did they even come in the house? You could clearly see the door had undergone a demolition from the street. He hadn't even made a trip to the back of the house to see if the close were clear. It was clear to them why Mona wasn't in an uproar or concerned about the safety of her children. She was under the influence. A pill head is what Serenity called her, but the streets called her a dem head. She was taking prescription pills. Sometimes she would mix her pills with Nyquil.

The Young and the Reckless

"Are y'all okay? Keith was dropping me off and I saw the lights on and I noticed the door gone. What happened?" Ms. Tina looked at Jackson waiting on him to answer.

Jackson asked Cameron to help him put Mona in the bed. Cameron told Jackson she could either just stay on the couch or lay in Serenity's bed.

"I know y'all will be glad when y'all daddy come home. He ain't going to have all this revolving door action and just maybe Mona will start acting like a mother." Ms. Tina pulled out her cigarette, lit it, and took a puff. She didn't care who feelings were hurt. Ms. Tina didn't know for sure about what was going on with Jackson. She did know that when he showed up, Mona's car was being vandalized and she was never home.

The police finally arrived, and Serenity told them that they just kicked the door down. She even went as far as saying it just happened and something had to run them off and they never got the opportunity to come in to get anything. Of course, one of the officers was a friend of Ms. Tina so he fixed the door without anyone asking him to do so after he dusted for prints. Before he left, he let Serenity and Ms. Tina know he would ride by more often and let other officers know to keep a look out. He continued letting them know he would drop the prints which he collected and off at the crime lab and as soon as he had information, he would inform them of anything he learned.

Jackson was useless. Mona had to think he was cute or something. Serenity had to admit he was quite a looker. He had a body like the Rock and face like Chris Brown. He sat back in the back like he was afraid, but most men in Serenity's neighborhood wasn't comfortable around the police. Serenity just felt as though Jackson would want them to be secure since he always had my mother in the streets as though she was some type of trophy. Serenity knew all that would be changing once her dad came home.

Serenity decided she need to call Que and let him know what had happened to her and her brother. She had been with Que for almost a year now. Things seem to be getting serious with them. She knew his specialty was trapping. She didn't know exactly what he was selling but she knew he was paid. She thought he was smart. He wasn't out flossing and stunting like most boys his age. He had a gray Honda Accord with a slightly tinted window. She heard he had a few bodies. But to her that was just hearsay. To her Que didn't have the characteristics of the gutter dudes she knew that were out in the street living life all reckless. He never told her, but the streets were always talking about him and his boys. They were from Walnut Park and everyone in the city of St. Louis knew how they got down. Serenity didn't know him at the time his parents were murdered. He had only told her about the tragedy he experienced once, and it was a few months in their relationship. She had gotten upset

The Young and the Reckless

with her mother and Cinque told her to shake it off. He went on to tell her you only get one mother so cherish it. As he let Serenity know about his loss, he barely made it through the story. They had been dating for almost a year and the only people that he was around that she knew was Kavon and Demond. She had no formal introductions. Serenity knew he had one sister and he lived with his uncle. As far as family that was all she knew of about his kinfolks. She only knew who his sister was and what she looked like from Star tagging him in a picture on his Facebook page. Que had one picture that he posted. It was a photo of the sky from the view of an airplane. One thing he did do was make it clear to her that he was living for the moment he could revenge their death. Que could have been the original writer for Omarion's song Ice Box. He literally had an ice box where his heart use to be.

CHAPTER 4

The most high sends the rain to fall and the sun to shine on the evil and the good. Today there were no obscurities in the energy of the universe. The sun was gleaming. It was as though the sun was smiling on Pharaoh giving him his on personal spotlight. Pharaoh cruised the city streets headed home. Shortly after cruising the city streets, driving slow enough to be seen by everyone, he pulled into his driveway. Pharaoh pressed the button on his garage door opener as it rested on his sun visor. He slightly pressed on the accelerator of his 2016 silver Mercedes-Benz S550 easing into the garage making sure his paint job went untouched by anything that could possibly be in the way. He had waited all week to pick up his car. Pharaoh had never drove the same vehicle no longer than two years. He was one that chose the lease option.

Pharaoh pressed the button again after he put his vehicle in park. The garaged door closed as he exited the vehicle. He looked back at his car and smiled. He could hear his brother Xavier criticizing him for choosing such a flashy car. As he entered the door leading to his home he said, "I wanted that

The Young and the Reckless

Bugatti Veyron Grand Sport, but I got make it out this community where there's no unity." He put those words in the atmosphere with the intention of responding to his deceased brother with hopes he had heard him. He popped the collar on his fresh white tee.

He entered his home realizing no one was there because it was way too quiet. Neveah would be either on Facetime with Paradise if she wasn't there hanging out. Either way their presence would be known and felt. They were not the usual teenagers that tip-toed around and kept secrets. Pharaoh knew all what they knew or, so he thought. He knew things about people he had no idea of what they even looked like. Well in person at least. Neveah and Paradise would pull up Facebook, Instagram or Snapchat and let him see who they were referring to. Cinque and his crew would be playing the PlayStation and making a big fuss about nothing. Either way he knew he was home alone. His house hadn't been this quiet in a while.

Pharaoh could afford to live in one of those exclusive gated communities and have a very expensive home with vaulted ceilings. He was content with his thirty-five hundred square feet four-bedroom home he resided in. Certain areas surrounding the St. Louis region has high segregation levels as though they are still stuck in the Jim Crow era. He didn't want to be one of those black families that had to worry about crosses being burned in his yard or having nigger go home painted anywhere on his property.

The interior of the entire home was painted a light smoke gray. All the ceilings were white with white moldings along the floor and the tops of the wall. There was wall to wall carpet except in the kitchen and three full bathrooms. The kitchen floor and bathroom floors possessed white marble tile. Each room had white up to date bedroom furniture. He called his living room the white room because everything from the sofa to the room accents were all white. This room would be the epitome of heaven, if it were all white.

The garage door lead directly into the kitchen. He entered the kitchen and headed in the direction of the refrigerator. He became distracted as he stopped dead in his efforts as he felt his cellphone vibrating against his side. He reached down and removed it from his cellphone holster. He pressed ignore because it was a number he didn't recognize, sending the caller straight to his voicemail. He continued his mission that he was on before he was interrupted by the phone call again. He reached out to grab the handle to the refrigerator and his doorbell rang. He looked down in his phone and seen it was his childhood friend.

When Pharaoh experienced the death of his brother and sister-in-law, he installed a top-notch security system. He was probably the first person who had a camera on his doorbell before most major security companies released it to the public. He headed to the door to let his friend inside. Pharaoh didn't know how anyone could take Torrance seriously. Torrance made sure everyone seen his perfect smile with his pearly white teeth.

The Young and the Reckless

"How you know I was home?" Pharaoh said to Torrance as he unlocked and opened the black wrought iron security screen door.

"What do you mean?" Torrance gasped with a look of confusion, "Dude, did you forget we just talked, and you told me to meet you at the house?" He followed Pharaoh in the kitchen and watched as he looked at his cellphone.

"This the third time this number has called me, and I don't know this number." Pharaoh watched as the number continued to flash across the screen.

"It could be Brittany. I see she is doing big things. She must have that bread. She just came back from Belize." Torrance smiled.

He decided to go ahead an answer. It could have very well been Brittany. She called him every blue moon and the last time she called it was from a 314-area code although she was staying in Arizona. He followed her on Instagram and knew that her magazine she created was allowing her to live her best life.

Pharaoh considered Torrance as his day one. They had been down for each other since fourth grade. Pharaoh and Torrance had been together through the good, the bad and the ugly.

The two of them met in Ms. Hamilton's fourth grade class. Ms. Hamilton was big on seating charts and every time she moved students around to keep from talking to one another they never seemed to be separated. When Ms. Hamilton posted the birthday, cupcakes labeled with the months of the year was the beginning of a lifelong friendship. Knowing that they both shared May fifteenth as their date of birth sealed the deal to their friendship. When YG rapped the lyrics to one of the tracks he did with Rich Homie Quan...

Know him since I was eight,
Fucked my first bitch,
passed her to my nigga
Hit my first lick....

My Nigga was their anthem that year it was released. Those lyrics described their friendship fully. Xavier was a big brother to them both. They all looked out for Torrance's little sister Tia. Torrance and Tia were their parents only two children. Juanita and Terry, Torrance's parents, were the owners of the most popular restaurant on the cities northside. Sweet Meals sold the best burgers in town. Torrance had eaten so many burgers, that the thought of them began to disgust him. Pharaoh was just the opposite. Burgers were his top choice. Burgers were the only thing this dynamic duo disagreed about.

"Hello." He paused as he was caught off guard. He listened to the voice come from the phone. He gave Torrance one of those I'm appalled facial expressions. He whispered, "this is a collect call from Nevaeh."

"Why would she be calling you collect?" Torrance was just as confused as Pharaoh. As far as he knew Nevaeh was pretty much a school scholar. Fashion, academics and hairstyles had

The Young and the Reckless

always seemed to be her focus. Then he thought about her best friend Paradise. They were night and day. Paradise was more like hell on wheels. He knew although Neveah was into her books, she and Paradise had to have some commonalities. Paradise growing up without her mother due to her dedication on her personal goals on becoming a physician. However, her grandmother was permanent fixture in Paradise's life. Paradise did have a dad who was very active in her life.

Torrance waited patiently to see how the phone call was about to unravel. He continued to watch Pharaoh as he nodded his head and only said okay. He wanted to interrupt but Cinque caught his attention as he came through the garage door with Kavon in tow.

"Who is he on the phone with?" Cinque immediately noticed his uncle's displaying a bewildered look upon his face as he entered the kitchen. He looked at Torrance waiting for his response. He asked out of curiosity because Pharaoh's facial expression and body language was sending out a bad signal. Pharaoh didn't do a lot of talking on the phone. He was worse than Denzel when he played Frank Lucas in *American Gangster*. Pharaoh let them know not on the phone constantly. That was part of the reason that Cinque didn't post his moves on Instagram or Facebook. Pharaoh was feeling like Tupac. All the eyes in the house were on him.

"Neveah." Torrance murmured.

Cinque and Kavon briefly glanced at one another as if knowing this was not going to turn out to be good outcome. He hadn't spoken with his sister in three days. He was glad this was their spring break. Pharaoh hadn't even tripped off the fact he hadn't seen his niece in the last three days. The way she and Cinque came and went, he didn't try to keep up with their whereabouts as much as he did when they were younger. Cinque knew he shouldn't have sent Nevaeh on what he was supposed to have taken care of in the first place. He had grown worried about her, but he had become distracted by Latrell's misfortunes. He couldn't let that issue ride. Latrell had nearly gone viral talking about how he ran off on his plug. Flashing a few stacks, shoes and clothes as he flossed on social media. His treacherous ways had a few guys spooked but no one had nothing to fear about him now. His days of backdooring his homeboys and anyone else were over.

"Raising children is more than material things. I really wanted better for you two. My plan was to show you all a different way. I have exposed you all to my dysfunctional ways and now my niece is sitting in a jail cell behind it. I know this is not what Bria and Xavier had planned for you all. I truly have blood on my hands." Pharaoh had everyone's attention. He had mixed emotions about Nevaeh being in a holding cell. He could only imagine she was dealing with the situation. He didn't know how he was going to even handle the situation.

Torrance wasn't for his friend's little guilt trip. Truth be told Xavier nor Pharaoh didn't have to go

The Young and the Reckless

the route they choose. They came from a two-parent home with parents who cared and worked every day. They did their best in school and were good enough to have a few scholarships to pay for their college experience. The way the street life dangled in front them appeared to be more lucrative. Torrance broke the moment of silence, "Aye man, what did she say?"

"Well you know she didn't say too much," Pharaoh was referring to the many conversations he had about never on the phone, "but they are holding them to build a case against Bernard. It sounds like he's about to be indicted. She and Paradise will be released on their own recognizance. They just trying to ensure that they appear for the trial in front of a grand jury. They towed the car but apparently didn't search it. She has to find out where they car was towed to so Torrance, I'm going to need you to go up there and wait for them to be released." Pharaoh waited for Torrance to respond.

Torrance nodded his head in agreement, "I got you." Was all he said letting Pharaoh know he was going to handle it. He didn't want any parts of an indictment. He didn't feel comfortable going anywhere near an individual that was on the authorities' radar. He was going to avoid bringing an unnecessary attention his way, but he was going to make sure Neveah and Paradise made it back to St. Louis. Pharaoh trusted Torrance with his life. He didn't want him to personally deliver Neveah and Paradise. That went unspoken and it was no need in speaking about how it was going to be done.

Pharaoh knew Torrance would get the job done. He always did.

Pharaoh turned and looked directly in Cinque's eyes, "Que, lucky for you it sounds like they didn't even search the car." He walked from in front of the sink from where he was standing and invaded Cinque's personal space. He placed his left hand on Cinque's right shoulder and the remaining hand on the remaining free shoulder. He began to tighten his grip on both of Cinque's shoulders. Cinque looked up slightly as his uncle stood over him. He was seeking to intimidate him, and it was working.

"Nephew, you know you have fucked up don't." Pharaoh had a firm grip on Cinque's shoulders as he spoke firmly looking directly into Cinque's eyes. He was looking at a younger version of himself. Although, he wasn't Cinque's father the genes of his very own father were very dominant. He had dreams of having children of his own but that was put on hold as he stepped out to take care of his brother's children.

Cinque stepped back yanking from the grip his uncle had on him. He looked over at Kavon who was not far from him to make sure he was on point. He began to address his uncle, "I'm a real nigga. I do this. In this game it comes with L's. I thought you knew this. Talking about you wanted different for us. How much work did you put in to show us different? My momma nor my dad never had me around no triple beams, paraphernalia beakers, and Draco's. None of that shit." He motioned his hand as he raised it above his chest moving across his chest

The Young and the Reckless

giving the cut off signal most comedians use to inform the DJ to stop playing the music. He continued, "You just said they didn't search the car. The way I see it they ain't got nothing on her. It looks like you and yo plug Bernard have the problem. Furthermore, we were never safe from this street life being around a nigga like you. We are not the same and don't forget that!" Cinque patted his chest, "I'm the realest nigga you'll ever meet. I love this shit lil bitch! You take this L as a lesson playboy."

Cinque left out the house. Kavon was right behind him. He couldn't believe how his friend had just disrespected his uncle. He didn't say anything. He waited for Cinque to speak. They entered Cinque's car and he sped off.

Pharaoh and Torrance stood looking at each other in disbelief. Pharaoh began to speak, "You heard what that lil dude just said to me. Torrance didn't know how to respond he was thinking to himself. "Dude, I'm standing right here with you. There's nothing wrong with my hearing and if you heard it, of course I heard it." He could tell Pharaoh was pissed and he wasn't about to help him take his anger to the next level by joking with him. He left as a thought as he looked away mildly shaking his head.

"I took him and his sister in my home. I taught that dude how to be a king in my castle. What man does that? He is walking around like Hugh Hefner in my shit. He just spoke to me real reckless." Pharaoh was on his Tyrese's what more do they want from me type of mission. The pain could be heard in his voice as he expressed himself. Cinque had never spoke to him in that manner. He didn't know how to deal with the disrespect.

Torrance looked at his homeboy, "He just caught his first body. He is feeling himself right now. Then he worried about his sister. He knows he shouldn't have had Neveah up in this mess. It's moving too fast for him. You know most people have four good years in this game before it comes to an end. We have been doing this for quite some time. It's time for a change. What dude tell Denzel in that movie?" He paused to think about the scene from the movie *American Gangster*, "quitting while you are ahead is not the same as just giving up. As far as Neveah, I'm going to drop a few bands on Tia and let her handle that so when she calls you back just tell her to hit Tia's line."

Tia is Torrance's younger sister. She has her own salon located near the downtown area of St. Louis. She specialized in all areas of hair. She could enhance the natural styles from locks to afros, install hair extensions which made the owner look like they grew the hair, but she loved the short a sleek. Fantasia made sure she came and sat in her chair whenever she came to St. Louis to perform. Fantasia's personal stylist didn't mind. Tia possessed the natural hair skills and a technique that many stylists admired.

Hair Fetish Salon was financed on behalf of Torrance. She was eight years older than Neveah, but she had been doing Neveah's hair before Bria and Xavier had passed. Bria and Tia were the only individuals who had ever touched Neveah's hair. Tia and Neveah had formed a special type of

The Young and the Reckless

relationship. Tia had been the big sister Neveah admired.

Pharaoh let Torrance out and locked up behind him. As he walked away from the door, he pulled his phone back out to call Cinque. He knew he had to make amends with him and it needed to be soon. As he was about to dial his nephew's number a call came through that put a massive smile on his face.

"Hey, Brittany." He didn't even say high. He wanted to immediately say her name. He knew women felt like they weren't being played if they heard their name or I love you. Other than that, they would feel as though the male was acting shady. It didn't matter who was in his presence, he said what he wanted, and people gave him the respect. Pharaoh name carried just as much as weight has John Gotti or Barack Obama in the streets of St. Louis. People who didn't know him respected him on the strength. He was a legend like Freeway Rick Ross the American drug trafficker. He was the new Mr. Untouchable of his era. He was the head of his own organized crime syndicate that controlled a significant part of the heroin trade in the Midwest. Ever since the death of his family he remained lowkey. He had no parts of the operation and neither did Torrance.

"It's been a long time since the last time we talked. You came across my mind and I said let me call the Emperor. I was little hesitant because I figured you were probably busy watching *Menace II Society.*" Brittany chuckled, and Pharaoh joined her. She enjoyed the movie just as much as he did. They had watched it a few times together. Pharaoh played the movie so much he didn't even have to sit in front of the television to know what was exactly taking place. He had worn Cinque and Nevaeh out with O-Dogg and Cain. Cinque and Nevaeh used to reenact the movie when they were younger and that just made Pharaoh's day.

"I actually watched it this morning before I went to the gym." Pharaoh said with a matter of fact tone. "I thought about you today too. I had an unknown number come up and I thought it was you with a new number. I thought to myself my queen has decided to be with me and she was coming back to claim what was rightfully hers." Pharaoh professed.

"I see you getting carried away. You keep trying your hardest to make me given into you. I'm may be down to give you what you want you keep it up." Brittany specified. She had been interested in taking it to the next level with him. She'd come up with a rebuttal with her thoughts about him that always stopped her. She had never heard anything about him being with several women. She just knew most wouldn't speak on it because if it got back to him, what they had would be over.

Pharaoh blushed, "Girl, we can act like two damn fools if you want."

"I'm ready and willing." Brittany shot back, "Before you be standing at attention, I want you to know I'm still in Phoenix. I'll be home this weekend."

The Young and the Reckless

"You don't have to get a room. You are welcomed to stay with me. Mi casa, your casa."

"Mi casa, su case." Brittany corrected him as he was trying to tell her his home was her home in Spanish. She continued, "that's cool. I don't want to impose upon your niece and nephew."

"Mostly likely they won't be her here, but it's up to you. Text me your flight information and I'll pick you from the airport." Pharaoh ended the call. He was glad Brittany had called him.

Pharaoh and Brittany had been friends for so long. She was there for him when he had been through the worse part of his life. His love for her hadn't change. Brittany just had so much going on in her personal life.

Brittany didn't have the typical life while growing up. Negativity had dominated her life and left her powerless. Her entire life, she felt as though every situation she was faced with worked against her. There was *No Limit* to what she was going to do to ensure her destiny had a positive outcome. She left St. Louis right after the Ferguson riots. It was believed that her and her friends robbed the check cashing place they had worked for, but the building was burned down to the ground during the riots. Now she was owner and publisher of *Taylor Made* magazine. She started off by writing blogs from the interviews she did with local comedians and underground artist. She went viral when she did an *exposé* on a young man on his way to college and was killed by an officer. Now she and her son were living happily ever after.

Pharaoh dialed Cinque's number. Cinque sent him straight to voicemail.

The Young and the Reckless

CHAPTER 5

Cinque brought the phone conversation he was having with Serenity to an end. He let her know he would stop by once he left from visiting with his grandparents. He parked his vehicle in the driveway of his grandparent's Staybridge Manor Parkway subdivision. His grandparents had a custom designed built home with the most stunning lake view. Every time he made this long drive he felt as though he was on some sort of vacation. The getaway of the city's hustle and bustle was often needed. The humidity he felt from the gentle breeze from the lake, he could tell summer was on its way. He walked up to the door and before he could knock or even ring the doorbell his grandmother opened the door.

His grandmother had been standing in the foyer of her home, looking out of the bay window which was next to the front door. She was the spitting image of the Late Lena Horne. Her silver sleek hair was pulled back into a bun. The pearl necklace she was wearing, lay on her slightly wrinkled skin elegantly. She was dressed like June Cleaver from the old tv show *Leave it to Beaver.* June cleaned her home looking as though she was headed to church in the seventies or eighties era. Although they had someone to clean their home for them, his grandmother lounged around her home dressed for any occasions. She and her husband often had dinner out or maybe a lunch date daily. They didn't stay in their home just letting time pass them by. They made sure if they were not traveling, they explored the entities of their community.

You could still see the beauty she once possessed in her youth. In her late sixties she was intact just like Angela Bassett. Margaret embraced him tightly not wanting to let him go. Cinque was the spitting image of her first born and she missed him dearly. She held him in her arms and before she released him, she exhaled.

"Come on in here and get some of this German Chocolate cake." She led him from the foyer into the kitchen. The kitchen was any chef's biggest dream. The vaulted ceiling was beautiful. In addition to the vaulted ceiling, the white cabinetry made the kitchen feel spacious. His grandfather was sitting at the breakfast bar reading his newspaper. He had his finger over his lip just as Xavier and Cinque did when they were deep in thought. Cinque walked over and dapped him up. He noticed his grandfather was a few pounds lighter since the last time he had laid his eyes on him. He didn't think much of his weight loss.

"Boy hug my neck. You haven't gotten too big for me to hug and kiss on you. It's been a month since the last time we saw you and Nevaeh." His grandfather put his newspaper down and forced him to hug him. As his grandfather embraced him

The Young and the Reckless

Cinque cried like a little baby. He had been longing for this moment for so long. He reminisced on the days that his father embraced him. He loved the way his grandfather showed him loved. Sometimes he felt as though he was connecting pieces of his dad, Xavier, when he and his grandfather embraced.

Xavier Sr. felt the tears was they fell. He heard the muffles and sniffles as Cinque tried to hide them. He could understand his pain. He lost a piece of him when his namesake departed. He began to speak as Cinque rested his head up against his chest, "Joseph Cinque was a West African man of the one of the largest ethnic groups in Sierra Leone by the name of Mende. Joseph Cinque led a revolt on a Spanish ship. He was captured illegally by the African slave traders and was sold. Cinque along with other Africans were tried for killing officers on the ship. He beat the case. He was found to have rightfully defended himself from being enslaved illegally. Your dad was impressed with the leadership he displayed. He had seen a movie by the name of *Amistad* and began conduct his research. He wanted you to stand out. He felt that you were unique. The moment you were born you had complications. You were supposed to be Xavier the third but the day you were removed from the incubator you became Cinque. You have a name to live up to. I care whether you live than die living up to the meaning of the name you were given, and you should too."

Cinque held on to every word his grandfather said. Cinque had his favorite type of cake and a full course meal during his visit. He wanted to go to the guest bedroom and just get some rest. He was surprised that his grandparents hadn't asked about Neveah. He had never been to his grandparent's home without her. It felt odd not being there without his sister, but he needed that alone time. He was seeking some sort of refuge from his uncle.

Cinque had only heard the story of his name twice in his life and the first time he was much younger. Hearing it today made him self-reflect. Children in his class would make jokes about his name and often his teachers mispronounced his name. He wanted to know why he didn't have a common name. His dad told him he didn't want him in his shadow. He wanted him to have his own name. He didn't want him to feel as though he had to follow in his footsteps. Xavier wanted Cinque's failures or successes to remain his own. Had he named him after him he would have been the third. Xavier thought having a new and unique name would be fun. Bria loved it, so she agreed. Cinque grew to love his name and every time someone mispronounced his name, he was sure to correct them. Sometimes he came off as arrogant during his corrections.

Cinque was enjoying the time he spent with his grandparents. He was glad he made the trip. He told a small white lie about Neveah spending time with her good friend Paradise on a shopping spree in the Windy City. Even though his uncle had three rules he said repeated throughout their life; Don't ever lie to him, don't tolerated disrespect from anyone and don't talk to me on the phone about anything that can be used against me in court, it

The Young and the Reckless

slightly bothered him having to lie to his grandfather. He assured his grandparents that he and Neveah wouldn't wait a month or longer to pay them another visit. Cinque said his goodbyes and headed back towards the city.

Cinque felt his phone vibrating. He pulled it out and quickly pressed ignore. He knew he needed to make amends with his uncle but today wouldn't be the day. He was mad at him and he couldn't explain the reason why. He was even mad at himself. Had he not been trying to push up on Star, Neveah wouldn't be sitting in a jail cell. Kavon was trying his best to convince him that it wasn't all his fault. He didn't know if Kavon was pressing him because he didn't want to go home. Kavon's dad had just come home from doing a five-year bid. He was having a hard time trying to provide for the family of four he had left. Kavon was pissed that his mom was being the man that his father needed to be. Kavon admired Pharaoh. He wanted to have the same admiration for his father, but he couldn't. His three younger siblings were glad their dad was home. He walked them to school and had even became involved with the parent teacher organization. Kavon felt that he was probably pushing up on the teachers and need to be pushing up on a job. He had even told his dad that Pharaoh could probably help him get on his feet. Kavon's dad let him know he didn't want any parts of Pharaoh's business.

Cinque was about to call Kavon up, but he decided against it. He called Demond up instead. He caught up with him. Demond was at the studio with

Davante and Hakeem. Demond let him know he would get back up with him once their studio session was over. He thought about heading over to the studio, but he found himself pulling up in front of Serenity's house. He was about to get out the car and go in, but he remembered the home invasion. He was thankful that he hadn't been there the night it happened. He had begun to slack off staying the night once he and Star reconnected. He wanted to make sure he was able to speak with her freely in the event she called him. Besides, he knew a couple of dudes would love to run up on him, so he called Serenity and told her to come outside.

Cinque listened as Serenity told him about the home invasion. The moment she told him about the St. Louis Cardinal tattoo on the hand, he knew immediately who it was. Now he needed to know what they were after. Cinque knew that her dad had left a few dollars behind. Serenity had told him all about that when they first met, but everyone knew Mona ran right through that. She could barely pay the bills. Serenity's grandmother was still sending money to them. Cinque was going to get to the bottom of this home invasion and he was going to the source. He tried to show some sympathy but was distracted when Star sent the "WYD" text message. He tuned in and out as Serenity spoke telling him about how scared she was and how her mother wasn't even concerned about the recent home invasion.

As the moonlight shone on Serenity flawless skin, he admired her beauty. He looked into her eyes and realized that he feared the moments to come.

The Young and the Reckless

He didn't want to break her heart, but he didn't want to lose Star all over again. He was between a rock and a hard place. She was oblivious to the fact that her number one spot was being replaced.

CHAPTER 6

Tia and Mason slowly pulled onto North Larrabee Street on the Northside of Chicago in her white on white Toyota Camry with legal tint. Mason was one of the older guys who worked for Pharaoh. Mason resembled the rapper Rick Ross. Not the old fat and chubby one but the one that was out here looking like new money. He was usually one of the enforcers of the crew. Today his job was to drive Neveah's car back to St. Louis. Pharaoh didn't want to take any chances with Neveah driving her car own back with the illegal substance it contained. Mason knew the risk that was involved but he was a loyal solider. He knew taking extraordinary risk came with the territory. Pharaoh had a lot of players in the game that looked out for him just the way Mason was doing. When Torrance reached out to Mason he didn't hesitate to help out. Torrance was selective in who he chose to accomplish certain task.

The weight that was in the trunk of Neveah's car had a street value of five million dollars. That was enough work for anyone to have a new start. Torrance selected someone who had been riding with them nearly since day one. Pharaoh and Torrance helped several individuals put food on their table. Mason was one of many that didn't have

The Young and the Reckless

anything on his record. His difficulty came with reading. There were not too many people that knew he couldn't read beyond a first-grade level. Who would know? No one gives you a reading test in the hood. He felt as though he could afford a little trouble had he encountered any. Mason knew his family would still be taking care of in the event he experienced any mishaps along the way.

Tia looked in the rearview mirror. She pulled her brush from the pocket of her Nike hoodie and freshened up her blonde waves. Tia's waves were better than most of the guys who brushed their hair every five seconds wishing for wave enhancements. It was as though she had spent twenty-four hours a day brushing her hair and sporting a wave cap when she found the time. You can find her brushing her hair as much as Joe Torry's character in *Poetic Justice*.

The barber in her salon had just hooked her up with a fresh haircut and she bleached her own hair blonde. She looked in her rearview mirror admiring her caramel skin as she and Mason sat waiting patiently on Neveah and Paradise to exit the police precinct. She looked in Mason's direction. He was resting his eyes, so she didn't turn the radio up loud as she was on a mission to listen to some music other than N.W.A. The rap group greatest hits CD that was on repeat as they made the drive to Chi-town. That was right up Mason's alley. He grew up on N.W.A. It wasn't new to Tia because her brother played it quite often. Tia began to scan through the radio stations as soon as she heard *Molly, Percocet, rep the set, gotta rep the set.* Neveah grabbed the car handle to open the door handle and snatched the door open.

"Chase a check. Don't ever chase a bitch!" Neveah rapped along to the song that was playing, smiling as she got into the backseat of Tia's car with Paradise in tow.

"You too happy for someone that just spent four days locked in a box. That's one hell of a way to spend your spring break. You didn't even get a chance to enjoy it." Tia started up the car, entered the address into her GPS. She waited on the directions to begin and made sure the traffic was clear before she pulled off.

"I know one thing. A bitch needs to bathe." Paradise sneered as she grabbed the rubber band she found on Tia's backseat and pulled her locks up into a bun. She had them twisted up into a nice neat bun. Upon her arrest the officers made her take her hair down to ensure there were no weapons are anything she could use to harm herself.

"It wasn't that bad. Those officers were actually pleasant. None of them had any rude demeanors. I am so surprised about the entire situation. We didn't get any mugshots taken nor were we fingerprinted." Neveah added, "I kept my mouth shut. I'm not sure of what happened to Sandra Bland other than she didn't make it out alive and I wasn't trying to have anyone saying my name with any hashtags. Too many of us are dying by the hands of those that supposed to be protecting and serving us. I was definitely not trying to go out like

The Young and the Reckless

Willy Lump Lump." Neveah laughed referring to the name she heard in the movie *Menace II Society*.

"I sure didn't want neither of us being included in the list of killings by law enforcement officers in the United States." Paradise added as she leaned back to get comfortable

Tia had a strange look as she turned to gaze at Neveah. She came to a complete stop at the red light, looked in her rearview mirror to check to see if they were being followed. She finally spoke, "That's strange. Did they ask for your ID or your name?"

Paradise didn't give Neveah a chance to answer, "They asked for Veah's identification when they first pulled us over and then came back for mine. They handed back both our IDs before they told us we were going to be detained."

The traffic light changed, and Tia made her way into the intersection. Halfway through the light Tia could see a black Ford F150 coming in their direction. She barely swerved out the way. It was in good timing. The truck missed them and struck the car which was behind them. Everyone slightly panicked and screamed obscenities as Tia drove away.

"I was about to take you all to a hotel, so you can have a chance to freshen up. I'm getting ready to take you all to this tow yard so you all can pick up your car. We need to get the hell out of Chi-Raq as fast as possible." Tia gained controlled of the car and headed towards City of Chicago Auto Pound. Tia's swerving of the vehicle interrupted Mason's brief nap. He opened his eyes to see what was going on. He looked back and noticed the traffic jam the accident had just caused. It was a minor fender bender it appeared to be no huge injuries.

Tia and Neveah entered the City of Chicago Auto Pound. Neveah gave the worker of the tow yard her ID and let the female know that her vehicle registration along with her documents for insurance were in the car. The female allowed Neveah to retrieve the items. Tia paid the fee, and Neveah drove the car off the lot to the street. Mason entered Neveah's green 2016 Grand Prix and pulled off.

Tia, Neveah and Paradise headed to grab a bite to eat. She couldn't leave until Mason let her know it was all good. If the packages from the plug was missing, he was instructed to make the car disappear. They were tucked in the inside lining of the trunk. You just couldn't open the trunk of the car and see them. The substance was packaged tightly and securely in green saran wrap. Tia looked down at her phone that was on her lap. Mason had texted her to let her know that nothing had been touched.

Paradise leaned up on the seat, "Let me see your charger. I know I bout got a thousand messages. Rome probably been blowing me up."

Rome's real name was Jerome. He was one of the young dudes that hung out on the set were Cinque's trap house belong. He was a street pharmacist that had a knack for stealing cars. As much as he stole cars, he was probably the reason no one called stolen cars stow-low's anymore, and the name was now box. Box could mean just about

The Young and the Reckless

anything simply because it contained things. If someone said pass me the box or it's in the box you would have to present to see what they were talking about. If you were listening in and wasn't supposed to be, you'd be lost in the lingo.

"I been thinking, and I just realized that you just turned sixteen. They probably didn't file any charges because y'all are minors. Did you give them your fake ID?" Tia questioned.

Neveah giggled, "I don't know what piece of identification I gave them. Truth be told, I was nervous. I kept my cool though. I wasn't even trying to finesse my way out of that situation. When you got dope in the car and the police gets behind you, your heart will stop. If I don't its sure feel likes it does." Neveah glanced out the window and was delighted about her freedom.

Paradise replied, "I was expecting them to be on some good cop versus bad cop type of shit. I was ready for they ass too. But they had us in a holdover cell together. We didn't say much of nothing if they were trying to listen. I was on my, I was built for this and couldn't be bought; rare but not average mission. I was ready for whatever they had coming for us. You know if Veah step, I'm coming ten toes behind her. Fuck they thought!"

Tia and Neveah looked at each other and snickered.

"What did my uncle say to you?" Neveah waited on Tia to respond.

"He didn't say anything. I only spoke with Torrance. I know he made a few calls. Then he gave me all the information on where you all were at and the car." Tia responded as she looked in her rearview and signaled to get over as she drove.

"I called my uncle and was trying to speak in codes. I was like me and Paradise came to Chicago to go shopping. We stopped by Unc house and he in some type of trouble. His trouble got us pulled over and they are taking us in for questioning. He wasn't saying nothing but mm hum and okay. I already know he didn't want me to say too much on the phone." Neveah paused and took sip from her drink, "Y'all just don't know how much this man had drilled me and Que about his three rules."

Paradise interrupted, "Don't ever lie to him, don't tolerate disrespect from anyone and don't talk to me on the phone about anything that can be used against me in court."

Neveah looked over at Paradise, "I guess you do know what he has said to us." They both laughed.

Paradise was the first friend Neveah had made when Pharaoh enrolled her in school. They have been together since 1st grade. Paradise lived with both of her parents and her grandmother. Paradise's mother was a Registered Nurse. She was working to become a Nurse Practitioner. She nor her mother had a problem with Paradise spending so much time with Neveah. Paradise's mom had taken an interest in Pharaoh. He was totally honest with her. He let her know that if they got involved, things may get ugly because he had

The Young and the Reckless

issues with commitment. He didn't want to be the reason behind Neveah and Paradise's friendship ending. He let her know he didn't want anything else taken from his niece. She respected his wishes. Although Paradise's father was present for her it was quite different for her mother. He had difficulty with monogamy. He didn't like the fact that she was so indulged with becoming a licensed nurse practitioner that it intimidated his general laborer position as a forklift driver at a local factory in the city. Her mother allowed him to remain in the home, so he could be there for Paradise. They thought their actions was in Paradise best interest. The love that they shared for one another was no more. Paradise knew but she pretended right along with them.

"I don't understand why my uncle does the things he does. He is like the hood hero and he doesn't even spend racks like he should."

Tia admired the way Pharaoh moved, "If you think about it, it's smart. People embrace and respect him. He has a lot of legal bread out here. I think he has like eight spots throughout the city. He has several rental properties. Your parents had a good insurance policy. So, I can honestly say he has his business affairs in order."

Neveah cut her off, "We are tripping. Those folks can be listening to us right now."

Paradise tittered, "This dude out here living like James St. Patrick. He may go eliminate his competition without anyone knowing he commits these murders." She referred to the fictious character from the Starz tv show *Power*.

"Nawal. He not out here like that. He moves totally different. Folks don't even know he the owner of those lounges. Kevin runs Midtown, Styles runs the Tap Room, Jessica runs Jessie's, Keith runs Imperial, hell I can't even think of everybody. I have only been to a few of those spots, but everyone thinks the people that runs those places is the owner. Once one got up and running, he would open another one. Robin helps him keep all that in order." Tia added. She knew about most of this from general observations from being around her brother. No one never just gave her the information, but she was smart enough to know what was going on. Just like she knew Pharaoh could never get caught up in being a crime boss. Nowadays he wasn't even going by the name Hot Rod. He stopped using the name shortly after Xavier passed.

"Let me call my brother and let him know I'm free." Neveah said, "Then I have to call Demond. I know he's just as worried but not showing Que how much he's worried about me." Neveah smiled thinking about how her brother approved of her seeing his friend. Demond had goals and aspirations. His rapper name D Savage. He put a few videos out on YouTube as was making a statement in the underground rap scene. Many people from his high school supported him and shared anything that he put out. The video that made him go viral was when he put the midget Luh Bill from the southside of St. Louis in it. He met Bill in summer school one year. He was making his own noise. The small person that stayed fresh in the latest gear. He was the joke of so many memes, but

The Young and the Reckless

he was just a first-year college kid with big dreams just like everyone else his age.

CHAPTER 7

"How's your granny doing?" Cinque asked waiting for Star to respond. He hadn't heard much about her condition since they had left the hospital. Her small gash was deep enough to receive stitches. For all he knew was that the people at the hospital had bandaged her up and sent her on her way.

"She's doing much better. It's my mom that's driving everyone crazy. She has this upcoming court date." Star stopped in mid-sentence. She had no plans on mentioning her mother's court appearance. She was testifying as a witness in a quadruple fatal shooting after a violent weekend in St. Louis City. "Everything is just so hectic and chaotic around this place. I needed that small getaway you had planned for us. I just want sometime where there are no responsibilities of everyday life that I have to deal with. Needing a break has long been overdue for me. I am preparing my sermon for this Sunday. This little spring break has gone by so fast. Next thing I know graduation will be here before you know it. What day is your graduation?"

"Umm... I think we graduate May 15th." Cinque was hesitant on talking about this date

The Young and the Reckless

because Serenity was already planning on attending his graduation. He had no clue to how he was going to handle this situation if Star wanted to attend his graduation. "How are you graduating this year? I recall you being a year behind me."

"I have met all my graduation requirements. My school has been through so many school counselors, my schedule has been jacked up since freshman year. I had classes with senior's my first year of high school. Any who, that's the same day as our graduation. Maybe we can plan something afterwards."

"Sounds good to me." Cinque was relieved he wasn't ready to break Serenity's heart nor tell Star she couldn't attend. He had never had to juggle two females before

"You should come visit my church. I'd love for you to come hear me deliver my sermon." Star had mad Youth Pastor at the church she had been attending at birth.

"You are doing another youth explosion. How many youth services do they have in one year? I see you on your Erica Campbell's *I Luh God* mission." Cinque guffawed loudly.

"It's better than being out here in these streets. The streets don't have no love for us. These city streets are so fake because love can get you killed and being killed gets you mad love." Star could understand why he was hesitant in coming to her church. She knew he didn't quite understand why his parents were no longer amongst the living. She knew there was no clear explanation of whys of life. She was just going to help him understand that it's okay to questions those whys. She knew he had a valid reason, but she was adamant on getting him back into the church atmosphere.

"The streets love me. I'm going be chasing the money until my heart stops." Cinque spoke with confidence ignoring the fact that Star was correct with her statement about streets having no love. He knew even more people would show him love when his heart stopped. He seen it happen to more than a few, "What you getting into today? I'm trying to see you today. Maybe we can go grab a bite to eat and see a movie. I want to see that new Ice Cube movie. Is it out yet?"

"I'm not sure what movies are out. My friends Davida and Nadia are coming over later. We didn't have anything major planned."

"Hey. Let me take this call. My coach is calling me. Look that movie time up and I'll take you and your friends on a date tonight." Cinque expressed himself with major confidence.

"Sounds good." Star agreed with her friends coming along. She wanted them to meet Cinque.

Cinque ended the call. He let Star know that he had a call coming through.

"Hey what's up, Coach Porter!"

The Young and the Reckless

"Cinque, what's going on. I'm just checking on my star player. Where are you? I'm trying to pull up on you."

"Pull up then. I'm on the block." Cinque was cool with his basketball coach. He had come into his life and became the positive influence he needed. Cinque admired his coach. He was young, black and educated. His uncle had taken him and his sister on many extravagant trips, but when his coach took him to Washington, D.C. to a Leadership Awards event the experience opened his eyes to a new world of opportunities. Following in his uncle footsteps took a backseat during the four days he was in the D.C. area with his Coach.

"You must have been around the corner when you called." Cinque questioned as his coach emerged from his red F150.

"Yeah. I was riding pass and I said let me call and see if he's out there." Coach Porter strutted up the steps to take a seat next to Cinque as he sat on the porch on the set of where he did his most work. Cinque was proud of his accomplishments on and of the field. He gave a signal to the lil loc that stood on the sidewalk not to far from the porch. He noticed the coach and knew what that meant. Cinque had the block hot and it wasn't even the summertime.

Coach Porter was from Missouri's Bootheel. He graduated college with a teaching degree but during his college days he was DJing for some hot artist who are making moves to get the top. He lists contained people like Young Jeezy an artist from Atlanta, Gucci Mane who is also from Atlanta and

Teresa Seals

Yo Gotti from out of Memphis. He moved to Atlanta and was staying with his friend from college who played for the Atlanta Falcons when he first graduated from Southeast Missouri State. DJing wasn't going as planned but his heart was still in it. He did odd jobs in between coaching for the private school Cinque was attending. He saw the potential in Cinque that he didn't see himself. Cinque scored a twenty-nine on his ACT and had mad skills on the basketball court. Pharaoh supported him in school, but he didn't give him the push like Coach Porter. Pharaoh only pushed Neveah academically. Coach Porter came into his life telling him about the positive opportunities he could be afforded if only he gave up the street life and pursed them. Porter was not giving up on him. Cinque became his little project. He was going to make sure he reached his full potential. Cinque had been exposed to the finer things in life, but Porter goals was to make sure he continued the lifestyle on a legal scale.

Coach Porter was one of the first teacher that showed him empathy instead of sympathy. Many teachers looked at him with pity in their eyes. Only one or two teachers knew the story about his parents. However, he became the topic of discussion in the teacher's lounge. They were several stories surfacing about him being a fatherless and motherless child. When he started hustling and went to school several teachers let him sleep. He missed half the work but was still maintaining a scholar's average grade. Coach Porter was big on forming relationships in and out of the schoolhouse. He even had the young lady he was involved with assisting. She was a law student

The Young and the Reckless

studying at St. Louis University. Porter's main goal was making sure everyone he encountered was productive citizens that could contribute and give back to those less unfortunate.

"You know decision day is May 1st. I'm not trying to find out what your decision is going to be, I'm just trying to ensure that you are going. I know you have a lot going on but this here street shit only leads to two places. I know it's an old cliché. This Tony Montana shit ain't for everybody. I just left a funeral of one of the young ladies that was trying to escape from a home invasion. You know I come from the country. It's slow where I come from this fast life is too fast for me. These people have no respect for living. A mother holds a child a safe within her womb. She's there to hold their child's hand in sickness and there to cheer them on being one of their biggest cheerleaders. I know you may not have your mother here with you physical but she's right here." Coach Porter tapped him on the chest, He continued, "Too many parents and families are being robbed. The streets are stealing and taking portions of many hearts. The streets are tearing souls apart. I know people are dying from diseases and other ailments but these streets having you creating your own deadly vicious circumstances. We need to be finding peace instead of trying to rest in it."

Demond, Kavon and Rome walked up on the porch. They all enjoyed being in the company of the coach. He could speak the street lingo and keep funky with getting it how you live the legal way. Demond started talking music with Coach Porter.

Rome let Cinque know that Paradise and Neveah were about to slid through. Cinque looked at his phone checking the text message Star had sent about the time the movie started. Cinque smiled when he seen Neveah's car pull up and Mason emerged from the vehicle. He knew it was time to stop ignoring his uncle calls and make amends with him. No matter how wrong his uncle could be, he always made it happen. He was with his uncle right, wrong or indifferent. He had to let him know it. Plus, he needed to talk with him about Serenity.

    Coach Porter said his goodbyes and headed to his truck. Cinque embraced his sister and kissed her on her forehead. He let her know he was about to go speak with their uncle. They all caught up and shortly afterwards they all left the scene.

The Young and the Reckless

CHAPTER 8

Pharaoh was having his house swept for hidden cameras and audio devices. This was done biweekly or as needed. As needed was when he and Torrance had to sit down and speak about their business. The professional he called had the highest-grade bug sweeping technology. They were a world class accredited sweep team corporation. After they finished, he would sweep right behind him spy guy device Neveah found him on Amazon. Once that was done, he was waiting on Torrance to come by. He showed up immediately when the sweep team left his home.

"Our shit just got here. Problem is what are we going to do when this is all gone. Our boy got bagged or getting bagged. We have to find a new connect." Pharaoh informed Torrance.

"I've been thinking about that and we need to come up with other transporting ways. It was cool having Que make it happen a few times but Neveah getting all caught up in this ain't cool." Torrance expressed his concern about the depraved decision that was made in putting her in this situation. He knew it was hard keeping the connect a secret and find people they could trust to pick it up their packages. It was time for a new way in getting their work.

"Yeah, I spoke with my boy Mike. He supposed to come up to the Midwest spot. You know I'm not for change, but I know we must change somethings. We've lasted in this game for quite some time and I've been thinking."

Torrance cut him off. The game had been good to them both even though they had experienced some losses, but he was not quite ready for it to come to an end just yet, "What's understood doesn't need to be explained." As he was about to start into his conversation Cinque walked in.

"What's up, Que!" Torrance dapped him up and he entered the kitchen, "I'm going to let you two men talk, hug, kiss and make up. Hot Rod, I will get up with you later."

Pharaoh felt weird being addressed by a name he hadn't heard it in years. It didn't sit right with him when Torrance called him that. Torrance knew it bothered him by calling him Hot Rod. Having a name that meant king or ruler fit Pharaoh well. Pharaoh was the name he now preferred, and his friend knew it. He played his part and was living up to according to the streets, but Torrance was ready for the throne. He was planning to let his friend know where he stood but today wasn't the day. He wanted him to make amends with his nephew.

"Unk, about the other day."

The Young and the Reckless

Pharaoh walked over to him and embraced him warmly, "No need to rehash that. I understand. Role models come in short supply. I can admit although I'm the realest you ever met, I've fell short." Pharaoh smirked.

Cinque chuckled, "I know what's understood, doesn't need to be explained. My coach came to through the spot today. I was thinking I'm going to go ahead and choose Purdue University on decision day."

"That's good! All this going on I kind of lost focus. I'm glad you didn't. I'm glad Porter came into your life. We all needed someone like him. I get pissed at my dad sometime for not being the man I needed him to be. Don't get me wrong, he was there but he didn't put his foot in our ass like we needed him to. He has never been the type to remind us of our wrongs. He just sat back and watch us do what we did. I can admit not having that made it hard for me to give it to you. Your dad was that man. I know he wouldn't want this life for you, but you remind me so much of him. I ain't gonna lie having you here with me, is like having him by my side." Pharaoh began to get teary eyed.

Neveah walked in and interrupted the sincerest moment Cinque and his uncle had ever had. "I'm home! Y'all missed me?"

Together they embraced her with a heartfelt grip.

"Did you get a court date? What did they say?" Pharaoh asked.

"First, they were talking about a federal indictment and then they were like sorry for the inconvenience we are going to let you girls go. I don't know what happened. I overheard them talking about a confidential informant, but I don't know personally what it was all about. I'm just happy I'm free and brother just know that was my last trip. The streets to turnt up for me. I got things to do with my life and jailing is not one of them. Uncle, you have sacrificed enough. You got enough money to be legit. You need to find you a good woman and go settle down. That G-shit old and played out. I know you got folks out here ready to ride for you but that squad not going to really hold you down. The minute things get bad they not going ride for you. Prison is for the birds and you are a lion. Hell, an eagle at least the way I see you. Out of all the homeboys that spoke about looking out for me and Que at the funeral haven't even kept their word. Only you and uncle T kept yawl word."

Pharaoh cut her off, "I get it Neveah. Just so you know Brittany is coming here soon. I told her she can crash here. So, why she's here we are going to live like the Cosby's. I feel you. I've been thinking about making new moves. It's time."

"Neveah, how is Paradise holding up." Cinque asked.

"She's good. She not worried about nothing but spending a few days with Rome before the rest of our break is over."

"I'm glad you good and home. I'm getting ready to hang out with Star and her friends."

The Young and the Reckless

"Star, from the old neighborhood." Neveah inquired.

Cinque smiled as he gave his head nod letting his sister know she was correct.

"That's what's up. Tell her I said hey. Does Serenity know you found you a knew friend." Neveah joked as she walked out, the kitchen.

"Playa, Playa. I see you nephew!"

"Let me go get ready." Cinque left his uncle in the kitchen.

He could hear Neveah talking on the phone.

"Who was that?" Cinque asked.

"That was Paradise. She is talking about she about to hang out with Rome. I ain't trying to go nowhere. I am going call Demond and see if he going to slide through to watch a movie with me, if he not in the studio."

Speaking with Pharaoh briefly left Cinque thoughts. He had to tell him about the situation with Serenity. When he went to speak with him, he was sound asleep.

CHAPTER 9

The sun was beginning to paint the sky with beautiful hues of radiant orange. The sunlight passed through the air as it began to rise. The birds were chirping a dawn chorus as though they were Destiny Child humming their tune *Cater 2 You.* Neveah grabbed her phone to check the time. Tia had told her she could come to the shop and she didn't have to worry about setting an appointment. Tia knew she needed to get some rest, so she let her know she could get in where she fit in once she arrived.

Demond had come through after he finished up with his studio session. As soon as the movie began Neveah was sleep. All she could remember was telling him about her jail experience, the movie starting and before she knew she was knocked out. She needed that rest. She barely got any rest during her brief incarceration. She was trying her best to listen to anything that was going on in the police precinct. She and Paradise talked majority of the time and tried to ear hustle for information to find out what was going on with their case. They were both looking for some leverage that could help them out. No news became good news and being released with no consequences was the best news.

The Young and the Reckless

Demond rose up as he could smell that breakfast was being prepared in the next room. Pharaoh decide to fix his niece and nephew breakfast. To his dismay Cinque hadn't come home. Demond and Neveah demolished the pancakes, hash browns, scrambled eggs with American cheese, turkey bacon and mimosas was what he had prepared.

Neveah walked in Hair Fetish Salon at noon. it was quite slow for a Saturday. She knew Tia had been there since 6 a.m. so she had probably did at least four or five heads. Tia and Neveah talked for a minute. They were interrupted when Torrance came in to get his hair cut by one of the barbers in the salon. They were tuned in to the conversations that were taken place.

All conversations came to a halt when the television displayed across the scene, *innocent driver killed when a stolen pickup flees police*. There was a black F150 banged up near a lamppost as a young man with dread locks was being handcuffed.

"Ain't that the lil dude that Paradise rocking with right now?" Tia asked.

"Yeah, that's the lil homie Rome and that looks like my homeboy Moe's F150. He came by the spot the other day and when he left, he saw his truck going down the street. Damn let me call him." Torrance remarked as he eyes stayed glued to the television as he pulled out his cellphone. Moe didn't have the regular F150. The chrome on the handles, grill on the front of truck, the bumper and the mirrors stood out like a sore thumb.

"Call Paradise and check on her." Tia demanded.

Neveah called Paradise's cellphone back to back with no avail. She began to grow weary with concern when she couldn't get in contact with her friend. She called Paradise's mother. She informed her they were headed to the hospital to see what type of condition Paradise was in at the moment from the car accident. They had no details of what had happened other than what the news was reporting.

Neveah called her brother. She let him know what she had just saw on the news. He told her he was about to make some calls and he would call her back.

Cinque sat on the side of the bed and began to flip through the channels. Everyone he dialed he received no answer. He stood up to wake Serenity up. He let her know it was about time for them to checkout and something had come up that he needed to handle.

Cinque had a busy night. He had taken Star and her friends Davida and Nadia out to eat and to see the movie Barbershop 3. He really enjoyed hanging out with the church girls. He thought it was going to be lame, but it wasn't as bad as he thought it would be. He had other needs that needed to be taken care of and he wasn't sure about how down Star would be. He called Serenity to let her know she was going with him for the night. Like always she agreed. She would do anything Cinque asked. He

The Young and the Reckless

didn't have a problem giving her few dollars, so she didn't have a problem satisfying his needs.

Cinque was in heavy rotation on this particular morning, he was like Blac Youngsta's song *Booty*. Nadia, Davida were on the phone with Star talking about how much fun they had with Star's new boo. As they were on the phone Nadia was scrolling through her Instagram and seen a caption that read...

That pussy put him in his feelings... #bae

She screenshotted the picture along with the caption and sent it to Davida. Davida couldn't believe it. All while the three of them were on the phone Davida and Nadia were having a sidebar conversation. They were trying to decide which one of them was going to tell Star. Ever since she seen Cinque outside the church during the youth explosion week that's all she seemed to have talked about. It had taken her thoughts away from the trial her mother was set to testify in soon. She had been so worried about the outcome of the case and what could possibly happen to her mother.

Star's mother had witnessed three young females murdered. She saw the shooters and could identify them both. The problem was the shooters were the nephew and son of the man she had been seeing off and on for the past seven years.

Moe was an older player in the game. Star's mother Patty was one of the many women he had amongst his stable. She happened to be on the street the same time the murders happened and a few hours later she was at the home with Moe when the murders walked in the door. Patty's good friend was a detective for the Saint Louis Police Department. She had just finished law school and was going to pursue her dreams of being a District Attorney. Star didn't care too much for her mother's friend, Shelly. She felt that Shelly used her mother as her own confidential informant. Patty stayed in the streets and that's right were Shelly needed her. Patty knew the who's who in the Lou. She knew Shelly used her, but she was using her as well. Patty didn't tell her about everybody. Quite as kept, Patty was one of the reasons Pharaoh name wasn't on the radar.

Moe was tall and thick glass of mocha latte with several tattoos. The one that stood out the most was the St. Louis Cardinal's red bird.

Moe had done a ten-year bid and while he was jailing, he heard about how Pharaoh was running the city. Before he went in there were a lot of players in the game but the way he heard, no one was seeing that bread like Hot Rod. He wanted to be down. When he figured out his homeboy was working for him, he eased his way in. He was only around Pharaoh when events happened like fights from Mayweather and concerts like the Hip Hop legends were on the scene. He knew about the façade Pharaoh put on about how he was making money, but he knew the truth behind those hefty insurance polices he cashed in on after the untimely death of his brother and wife.

Pharaoh was the beneficiary of two hefty insurance policies. He was a respected business

The Young and the Reckless

owner that played the background. He tried to stay away from the vultures and scavengers that preyed upon the sick or wounded. However, the city of St. Louis is just like any city where people split your wig to get what you have worked so hard for just to get to a higher ground. Pharaoh knew that and that was one of the reasons he had a modest home. It was different when it came to his cars. He would splurge a little. Moe understood why Pharaoh lived the way he did, and he respected it. At least while he was in the presence of Pharaoh.

Davida came to the decision it would be her to break the bad news to her friend. She decided that she would send Star the image of Cinque in the arms of Serenity as his head laid between her exposed cleavage.

CHAPTER 10

Dion, Patrick and Andrew pulled into the driveway of Dion's home. As soon as they reached the front door Dana the female, they had just met at West County mall had phoned him. West County Mall was in the suburb of St. Louis county. The mall was centrally located and was most famous for the large dove sign which sat outside the mall's main entrance near the interstate. Countless sorts of socioeconomics statuses could be found frequenting the mall. This was one of the reasons Dana often chose to patronize this particular mall.

Dion had just moved in to his first home. He was renting from his uncle but it he considered it his. A starter home on the city's northside which sat tucked away near Highway 70 and North Grand Avenue. He chit chatted as he walked into his home with his two friends in tow. Before he ended the call, Dana had agreed to come over. She had taken a notice to the stacks they were spending in the mall. Dion had purchased three different Nike air max 97s when she walked into Footlocker. Him spending six hundred dollars on three pair of shoes caught her attention. He pulled out his stash with no problems. Patrick and Andrew had a few shopping bags, but

The Young and the Reckless

Dana had her eye on the one that appeared to be on boss status.

Dana had knocked on the door and Andrew let her in the home. He let her know that Dion was in the shower. Patrick began to have small talk as Dion weighed marijuana on small scale as he sat at the kitchen table. Dana could see into the kitchen from where she sat on the latte colored sofa. Patrick complimented Dana's large box braids and asked her about some friends she could call over to join her. Dana pulled out her phone. She asked Patrick for the address and she repeated the address to the friend she had on the phone.

Dana asked what was taking Dion so long. Patrick stood up to go check before he could leave the room there was a knock at the door. Patrick went to open the door and tried to run when he was looking down the barrel of a semi-automatic weapon. He was gunned down before he made to the kitchen where Andrew sat at the table with bags of marijuana.

Gordon Perry asked Dana how many were in the house. Dana gave the hand signal for three. Andrew reached for the backdoor as Robert Jackson continue to unload his automatic semi weapon. Dion heard the gunshots and as he tried to escape out the bathroom window Gordon stopped him dead in his tracks. Gordon and Robert raped the house with the assistance of Dana. Three black hefty trash bags were at the door. The bags contained at least twenty pounds of marijuana, an unknown amount of cash he had grabbed from the top of closet in the bedroom that housed the items

Dion had just purchased from the mall. He took those items too

When the police arrived at the scene, they found five bodies. Gordon left Robert and his girlfriend Dana with the guys they saw dropping stacks earlier in the mall. When Dana made the call, Gordon had already made the decision he was going to be the last man standing. He called his cousin Mario to come assist him in his wrong doing.

The blanket of gloom hung amongst the shining stars in the sky. There was no sound of silence. An orchestrated screech of overpowered humming from the cicadas amplified the vrooms of engines revving as motor vehicles operated at high speeds down the busy boulevard. Patrons poured into the Midtown. Kevin made sure the drinks were coming to the table were Torrance and Pharaoh occupied. They were having a mild celebration after meeting with Mike. He told them what they wanted to hear. They didn't have to worry about any more trips to Chicago. What they needed were going to come to them.

Moe parked his black F150. He exited his truck and took a look at himself in the tint. His little Boosie fade was on point. He smiled giving his six-foot frame his own signature of approval. He walked in Midtown an immediately notice Torrance and Pharaoh. He was patted down and searched by Midtown's security. Nothing was found on his person, so he had approval to enter the lounge. He walked over to join them. Torrance and Moe had a

The Young and the Reckless

better relationship than Moe and Pharaoh. It was something about Moe that didn't sit well with Pharaoh. Moe felt uneasy, so he didn't stay long. He paid for the one drink he had and pretended to receive a call that cut his night short. Moe spoke with Kevin briefly and then he walked out the door of Midtown. He watched as his F150 drove away without him in it.

Moe's entire mood had changed. He was already feeling uneasy. He was mad at himself for not following his first mind. Had he put his truck in the shop from the minor fender bender he just encountered he would at least still be in possession of it.

Moe didn't even reenter in the club. Moe text Kevin to let him know someone had just stole his truck. Pharaoh and Torrance came out and noticed him standing there. He let them know what was going on and Torrance offered him a ride home. Moe agreed.

Torrance pulled up in front of Moe's duplex. Torrance asked was he cool because it was a guy dressed in all black sitting in the chair on the porch. Torrance knew his son was in jail awaiting trial along with Moe sister's son. He had been around Moe long enough to know some of the people in his family.

"That's my little cousin Gordon. His mother out here on that shit so I let him crash at my spot. He probably just sitting on the porch smoking. You know I have rules and they are the same rules my mom had while I was growing up. He can't smoke in the house because of mom's oxygen." Moe thanked

Torrance for the ride and told him he would get up with him later.

    Torrance asked him did he think the Cardinals were going to make to the World Series. Everyone knew Moe was a huge Cardinal's fan. He had the red cardinal bird tatted on his hand just to show how far his loyalty went with the St. Louis Cardinals. His grandfather was a true fan. He would listen to the games on KMOX when Jack Buck was the announcer. His grandfather died shortly after Jack Buck in 2002. Moe had lost the one person who genuinely loved him. He never learned how to conquer the most painful lost he had ever experienced. The self-doubt set in and he never found the one person to empower him to be courageous and live a fulfilled life.

The Young and the Reckless

CHAPTER 11

Paradise practically praised danced to show just how much she was grateful to be and free. The past four days had been awfully weird to her. Paradise was glad to be released. She was glad to finally be home and spend some quality time with some of her loved ones again. Just a few days ago she found comfort in jailing with her best friend Neveah not knowing her fate. She knew if that jail experience would had been a huge difference if she and her bestie were apart.

Paradise knew she wouldn't have been able to survive the stint had she been alone. Even after they were freed, she still didn't understand why they were detained in the first place. It was quite confusing that Neveah was the only one allowed to make a phone call, but she had no one to call anyway. She would have given her father, mother and grandmother a heart attack had they heard someone telling them they had a collect call for her.

Paradise had more freedom than most fifteen-year-old girls her age had. She had a mother who was working hard to give her a better life and a grandmother who was old enough to be knocking on heaven doors. Along with a father who worked many hours to have the cash flow her mother had been maintaining. Paradise's mother, Beatrice was in the last two years of her medical degree. She was now with other students interning working directly with the patients under the supervisor of experienced doctors. Nurse Practitioner degrees usually takes two to four years, but it was taking Beatrice nearly six. She had to take some time off from school when her mother had a stroke.

Paradise retrieved her cell phone and pulled up the Pandora app. Scrolling through the stations she placed it on the Anita Baker station. It was a station her mom always listened to, so she was familiar with the songs that were in rotation. After locating her station, she then got ready to bathe.

Paradise had bathed for an entire hour. As she soaked in the tub, she had to turn the hot water on a few times because the water began to become frigid while she soaked. She eventually stood up and turned the shower on to wash her long locks. She called her mother to see how she was doing. Her mother was glad to hear her voice. She wasn't expecting to hear from her while she was on break. Beatrice figured that she was with Neveah as usual. Once off the phone she went to check on her grandmother. She spent a few minutes with her grandmother and she brushed her silver hair that was soft as cotton balls. Her grandmother slurred a few words. She had gain mobility throughout her body, but her speech was taking its time to return. She wrapped up her time with her grandmother and headed to her room.

Paradise grabbed her finger nail polish and began to polish her toes. When she was done, she

The Young and the Reckless

decided to call Rome to see what he was up to. Rome was doing what she figured he was doing. He was outside posted like a lamppost as he hugged the block as usual. Paradise began to fill him in on her four-day bid.

Rome listened. He didn't know what to think. He couldn't understand how they got out, but he did understand how they were pulled over on some bogus mix up. He cracked a joke about the arrest and changed the subject.

"You think I can see you tonight?" Rome asked hopping she said yes.

"As long as you come get me." She replied.

"Aw. You ain't said nothing but a word. Give me an hour and I'll be on my way."

Kavon pulled up on the block. He parked to check out the scene. He saw the usual faces. They had paused from their drug dealing activities or shooting the breeze with conversations checking to see who had pulled up. Kavon saw the one individual he rocked with when he was out on the block. He got out and walked up to Rome asking had he seen Demond or Que. Rome let him know that Demond had just left and it had been a minute since he had seen Que. Then Rome asked Kavon for a ride to his ride. Kavon knew exactly what he meant. Rome need a ride to accomplish his criminal act of motor vehicle theft.

Teresa Seals

Nationwide in the United States there is roughly over seven hundred thousand motor vehicle thefts within a year and Rome contributed to these numbers at least three times in one week.

Kavon maneuvered his way through the traffic. The city streets were heavy populated. The warmness of the night had just about everyone out. Police and ambulance sirens could be heard in the distance amongst the hustle and bustle. A crowd of motorcycles bombarded the flow of the northbound traffic on Natural Bridge. Black leather vest with eagle wings on an individual which was on a motorcycle with the monument St. Louis was best known appeared in the background glared from behind raised handlebars. They were performing stunts and playing loud music. Riders on illegal dirt bikes and ATV's were gunning down the city streets amongst the bikers and the car cruisers.

Dusk had settled, the moon was full, and a significant amount of public nuisance was taking place. If you listened hard enough, you could her people using foul or abusive language. The young at heart were out having fun. After turning a few corners Rome saw his vehicle.

"Slow down." Rome uttered to Kavon.

"You sure want one of these cars around here. You know this is one of Pharaoh's spots." Kavon warned Rome. He tried to convince him that he was not making the best decision right outside of Midtown.

The Young and the Reckless

"I'm not about to hop in Pharaoh, Torrance or Kevin's ride so it's all good."

Kavon came to a complete stop. Rome dapped him up and exited the vehicle. He walked right up to the shiny chromed out black F150. He walked around and noticed it had been in an accident. The truck wasn't beat up too bad, but it needed some minor work. He pulled the handle and the door open right up. He smiled at Kavon. He hopped in the truck with his big screwdriver and bust the tumbler out of the column. The truck cranked right up. Kavon pulled off and Rome pulled off behind him.

As he approached the intersection of St. Louis Ave the light turned red and he kept going. He drove cautiously doing the speed limit. He was trying not to attract unwanted attention. He was headed to see his girl.

Rome pulled up in front of Paradise's home. He exited the truck and walked up on her porch. When he made it to the door, he pulled up his black Nike sweatpants. He took his hand to dust off his hoodie that matched his pants. He started to ring the doorbell, but he decided against it. He sent a text message to let her know he was at the door. She came right out.

Rome headed back to the block with Paradise right by his side. When he got out the car, she noticed there were no keys in the ignition. She just shook her head and smiled. She scanned through her phone as Rome made a few sales. He walked up to the window of the truck and she opened the door. He moved back to ensure she was not about to hit him with the door of the truck.

"You are staying with me tonight." Rome asked looking for confirmation of how his night was about to end.

"Are you asking me or telling me?" Paradise blushed as she inquired about Rome's question, "I may not have a choice being that you got me in this truck you have borrowed."

"Let me make a few more sales and then we out of here." Rome walked away from the truck and Paradise closed the door.

In less than twenty minutes Rome was back in the truck and headed towards the Western Inn motel. He got a room for forty-six dollars that he didn't have to show any identification. Once inside the room, Rome cut on the air condition to cool off the stuffy room. The room was clean with out of date furniture. Everything from the lamps to the flat screen tv were mounted down. Rome went to the bathroom. He had to wash the hustling stint off. Paradise laughed as he pulled his toothbrush, Degree deodorant and fresh pair of Ethika boxers out the gray and orange Adidas bookbag she didn't see him with until he had gotten out the truck.

Rome posted up right up under Paradise. They had several rounds of foreplay before they were completely undressed and exploring one another souls.

The sounds of housekeeping knocking on the other doors woke them up. Rome stood up from the

The Young and the Reckless

bed to see what was going on outside of their room. He looked at the time and it was after checkout time. He and Paradise showered together and dressed in the same attire afterwards. He let Paradise know he had to handle a few things, turn a few corners then he would take her home.

Rome pulled on North 20th Street and East Grand Boulevard and hopped out the truck. He served a few customers with some grams of his loud. Loud was different from the regular marijuana. It had a smell that applied pressure to the nostrils. The stint was loud hence the name. He hopped back in the truck and seen the police cruiser in his rearview. He sped off and the cruiser put up chase. He was headed south on Grand. He turned a few corners and lost the police cruiser. When he turned the corner, he bumped a navy-blue Nissan Sentra. The Nissan blocked the intersection and the cruiser couldn't make it pass the Sentra without interfering with the oncoming traffic of the southbound lane.

Rome and Paradise laughed and talked as though they had hit the six winning numbers to a three million-dollar Powerball. Getting away from the police and leaving them stuck in traffic brought on an adrenaline rush.

"Fuck the police!" Rome exclaimed.

As soon as he finished his statement, he looked in the rearview and seen three more police cruisers. He led them on a chase.

Right as they approached Natural Bridge and Newstead, they were headed to turn to lose the cruisers that were behind them. Instead of the silver SS Impala stopping at the red light, they were coming at high speed and crashed right into the Impala. The impact threw Paradise from the car. Paradise was under the truck and Rome was knocked unconscious. The driver of the Impala died instantly from the impact. The pedestrians on the street ran together to shift the truck off Paradise. Paradise was rushed to the hospital and Rome was handcuffed. Gordon Perry, the driver of the silver SS impala, died on the scene.

Gordon Perry experienced what some like to call karma. Two days ago, he was out on a mission to make sure he was able to feed his drug habit. At the age of twelve he was smoking marijuana and by fifteen he was popping pills. Due to the fact so many children were overdosing on prescription pills, laws began to be created to hold drug distributors responsible. The pharmaceutical companies started cutting back on supplies, but the street demand only increased. Gordon slowly began to use heroin. In more affluent communities' children were given alternative methods to rehabilitate their drug use but, in the hood, it just went ignored. Families members often were ashamed, so they found to easier to not deal with the individual. Like many Gordon found himself to be more accepted by likeminded individuals. Hence making the old saying birds of a feather flock together cliché seems to be only an understatement. When nine times out of ten some individuals only use drugs to relieve the pain they were undergoing. The pain could have been caused by several unknown factors. The dope man was easier to seek than a psychiatrist.

The Young and the Reckless

Gordon's checkered past had caught up with him quick. The nineteen-year-old boy had cut the lives short of five individuals. He didn't live long enough to spend all what he had stolen. All his stolen goods had done was provide the payment for his funeral. His family didn't have to set up a go-fund me page or do any fundraising events to bury him. For some strange reason most people didn't have life insurance. They literally couldn't afford to die. One can assume that people do see the need until tragedy strikes. But if you stay ready for the unknown you don't have to get ready when an unexpected tragedy knocks on the front door.

Gordon Perry was a thing of the past his dash between his birthdate and death date didn't have much to say. He hadn't left much of a mark on the world, but you couldn't tell by all the individuals who attended his homegoing ceremony. There was standing room only. Family members from near and far paid their respects. His life may have been so much more had he been shown the same sort of love long before he turned to the streets.

Neveah watched along with Tia and Torrance as the news reporter recapped the details of the accident. Paradise's name was withheld but Rome could be seen being escorted from the ambulance in handcuffs. The news reported how one victim was pinned under the F150 and the community came to the rescue. She knew it had to be her fiend or she had to find out if it was her before she panicked not truly knowing if it were Paradise or not. Paradise's mom confirmed it was her the new reported mention as the other victim. Neveah found out what hospital she had been taken to. Tia drove Neveah straight to the hospital. She was too shaken up to drive.

When Tia and Neveah reached the waiting room they were met by Cinque, Kavon and Demond along with Paradise's mother. Beatrice was having a hard time trying to contact Paradise's father. She left him a voicemail in hopes that he would get it.

Pharaoh came through the hospital door. He embraced Neveah and then went to comfort Beatrice. Torrance had called him and brought him up to speed with what had happened to Rome and Paradise.

Things were quiet for the moment. Neveah paced the floor. Demond was in his phone scrolling through Facebook and Instagram. He discovered a picture that his friend was not going to be pleased with at all.

"Look like you, Paradise and Rome are trending topics." Demond sneered. He seen so many people sharing and tagging pictures of the destroyed F150 and Impala. He walked over to show his homeboy the picture of him laying on a set of scrumptious breasts. "Dude, your picture doing numbers. This mug has been shared nine hundred times."

"Damn, I'm sure Star has seen this by now." Cinque became furious. He was about to go berserk. He was pissed with Serenity instantly. He couldn't believe she posted that picture of him. He had discussed with her several times about not having

The Young and the Reckless

his face being on social media. Cinque had turned into the mad hatter. It was though he was foaming at the mouth and his lips were tight trying to keep the liquid from seeping out. Everyone in the waiting room became distracted by the group of doctors which were approaching the waiting room. Pharaoh stood with Beatrice as the doctor who had appeared to be the oldest of the bunch began to speak.

CHAPTER 12

The hospital waiting room was with silence. Every once in while a sniffle or sigh from weep could be heard. Tia sat on the floor with her legs crossed as if she had mastered the science of Yoga breathing and meditation. Kavon was sitting directly across from Tia in one of the padded floral pattern chairs that occupied the waiting room near the vending machine. Neveah had her head resting on Demond's chest as he sat next to Kavon. Pharaoh would go from sitting to standing. He was attempting to comfort Beatrice who was pacing the floor of the waiting room. He didn't want Paradise's father to come and interpret him comforting Beatrice as more than what it was. She would weep and then fuss about Paradise riding in the stolen car with Rome. Her eyes were swollen from all the crying she had endured. Beatrice wore an exhausted weary look upon her face. Cinque was glued to his phone. The group to support Paradise were spread about as if they were camping out. They were in the waiting area amongst themselves

Cinque had dialed Star's cellphone twelve times since he had been sitting waiting to hear a word about Paradise's condition. He could tell she was sending him straight to voicemail. He was not about to leave a message. He didn't even know what to say. All he knew is that he didn't want to appear

The Young and the Reckless

to be guilty and the relationship to end before it even started. Her ignoring his calls and sending him to voicemail made him believe that Star had to have seen the picture by now. With over nine hundred shares it was impossible for her to have not seen the picture that Serenity posted. Memes and several captions were on the shared photo. Cinque wasn't fond of any of them. He logged off social media and opened his text messages. He sent the WYD text message. Star received the text. She was not trying to tell him about what she was doing. She left him on read.

  Everyone who was in the waiting room were either aggravated about not knowing the outcome or anxiously waiting out of concern about the state of the condition Paradise was in. Finally, a few white coats came back walking slowly down the hall. They didn't have much news about Paradise the first time they came to greet them. Earlier the doctors were just introducing themselves letting Beatrice know who would be working with her child.

  Three males and two females approached the waiting room. Each doctor took time to explain in detail their title and their work capacity with Paradise's condition. In front of them all stood one anesthesiologist to numb Paradise's pain. The cardiologist was there to monitor her heart. An emergency medicine specialist to make the life-or-death decisions for her injuries. The neurologist which was there to support her brain, spinal cord and nerves. Then there was a plastic surgeon to rebuild or repair her cosmetic needs. The entire room accepted the greetings from the doctor. They were past the point of introductions and job titles. They wanted to hear about Paradise. Beatrice let them know that she was the patient's mother. She was totally in mother mode. She was attentive and concerned about the well-being of her only child. The apprehension was written all over her face. She was fighting back the tears. The doctors came with more information than they had the first time.

The eldest physician of the bunch was with prematurely grey hair noticed everyone were tuned in ready to hear play by play of either the results or the condition. He was the medicine specialist. "You have a survivor of a head on collision. I'm not sure if you are aware that Paradise was ejected from the vehicle. On top of being ejected from the vehicle it then landed on top of her, pinning her underneath the exhaust. We hear that the onlookers pushed the vehicle off her. Things could have been a lot different if they hadn't been there to lend a hand. Her fibula and tibia of the left leg were fractured. She is pretty banged up. Those scrapes and bruises she endured will heal in due time. Does anyone have any questions of us?" the physician with prematurely grey hair concluded as the other physicians stood around nodding giving confirmation in what the doctor had stated.

Pharaoh looked down at his phone. Brittany had sent him the text message he had been waiting on. He smiled when he saw that Brittany's plane was about to land. He looked up from his phone. He asked the first and only question, "When can we go back to see her?"

The Young and the Reckless

The doctor let them know she needed her rest and at the time only two at a time could go back to where she was located. Everyone agreed that Beatrice and Neveah would go back first.

Pharaoh sent his love and let them know he was headed out. He pulled Neveah aside stopping her from going back as though he had top secret information. He let Neveah know he was headed to the airport to go pick up Brittany. Neveah gave him a smile and he knew she was simply wishing him well. He knew that she was more worried about the condition of her best friend whether being concerned about his love life. He couldn't wait to see the one individual who held the key to his heart.

Pharaoh hopped on interstate 40 taking it to interstate 170 headed to St. Louis Lambert Intranational Airport. He made his exit and parked at Cell Phone Lot Terminal 2. TSA didn't allow individuals to sit and wait for passenger pick up right outside the airport. The wait terminals were created post 9-11. Airport checkpoint screening significantly tightened. Two months after the attack, Congress federalized airport security by passing the Aviation and Transportation Security Act Transportation Security Administration took over all the security functions that previously took place.

Brittany sent Pharaoh a text message to let him know that she was about to grab her luggage and stand outside. Pharaoh text back.

I'm in a silver car.

Brittany looked at her phone and said to herself, "I hope he has the only silver car out here."

When she came out, she saw Pharaoh waving his hand. She walked towards him pulling her light blue hard side luggage with wheels.

"Dude, you could have said, I'm in a silver Benz!" Brittany exclaimed.

Pharaoh walked over to her and grabbed the luggage, He then placed it in the trunk of his car.

"You packed light."

"I will probably go shopping and just buy me another suit case to take my stuff home."

"How's lil man?" Pharaoh inquired about her son. He knew her son spent an enormous amount of time with his paternal grandparents.

"He's fine. He's here in St. Louis. So, I'm going to go see him while I'm here."

Pharaoh thought it was quite odd that her only son spent more time with his paternal grandparents than he did with her, but he was not going to be judgmental. He was willing to accept the package deal if they were to take it a step further.

"Are you hungry?" he inquired.

"Yes! I was just about to tell you that I want some Imo's, Chinese food, or White Castles" Anytime anyone moved away from St. Louis those were the three food items they missed the most. Brittany looked at him awaiting his response.

The Young and the Reckless

Before he could respond she had more to say, "I wanna try those Red Hot Riplet wings from that chicken place out on Manchester Road."

"I haven't tried those wings. You know what the place is called. I keep hearing people talking about, but I've never been."

"Let me ask my Facebook friends. That's how I know about the wings in the first place." Brittany posted to her page asking about the name of the place that sold the Red Hot Riplet wings. She then sized Pharaoh up. He was still fine to her. He didn't have on nothing special, but he still looked nice. White tee and grey sweats were his attire. She couldn't see his shoes, but she assumed they were sneakers.

Brittany received several replies to her post. She told Pharaoh where to go. He placed the address in his GPS and head to St. Louis Wing Company. Once there he parked. He exited the vehicle and walked around to open Brittany's car door. She looked down and noticed he had on some Salt Yeezys. She couldn't believe he bought those shoes. She was going to say something about it later.

The two of them entered the restaurant and placed their ordered. They then took a seat to wait on their food. Pharaoh brought Brittany up to date about what was going on with Neveah's and her close friend, Paradise. Brittany let him know how good her magazine was doing on the west and east coast. She had plans to look for new territories to conquer. The south was next on her list. Their food was eventually brought to their table and the small talk ended. The food now had their undivided attention.

The Young and the Reckless

CHAPTER 13

Reconnecting with Star had Cinque feeling somewhere between happy and satisfied. He was overjoyed to say the least. He hadn't been so happy in quite some time. He never wanted that tranquil feeling he experienced with Star to end. He was enjoying the vibrant beauty she displayed vividly. She was good for him and he knew it. He tried not to compare her to Serenity. He was trying to forget she even existed even though it would become one complicated situation with Serenity. He had plans to apply major pressure to his situation with Star. She was going to feel that heaviness he carried in his heart for her. He spent the entire night pondering on how he was about to make Star know he had taken an interest for her on a deeper, intimate level.

Kavon looked at Cinque and held on to every word he heard him say. Cinque stated to him you should never display that you are not loyal to your real true love. Kavon knew right then his friend had to be really feeling Star. He realized that there had to be a strong attraction or and emotional attachment towards her. He looked over at the church they had parked in front of and looked over at Cinque. Kavon knew that this Star had to be a big deal. He had never seen his friend like this before.

He almost didn't recognize him. In love was a good look for him Kavon thought. He was waiting on him to take the lead.

Cinque led the way into the Mt. Pleasant AMC. He was glad that Star had shared her location with him on the night he took her and her friends to the movies. He used the location app on Sunday morning to see where she was. He had been checking her location every time she ignored his called and left him on read. He was pleased to see that she was either at home or at church.

The usher standing at the door handed both of young men the church program. The usher was an elderly woman who proudly wore a gold button up oxford shirt with the Mt. Pleasant AMC embroidered in black on the left side of her shirt with a black pencil skirt. Her stockings were loosely hanging around her ankles, but she moved about as though she hadn't noticed. She was a petite gray-haired woman who smiled and directed the members as though she was Kirk Franklin get ready to pump up a gospel choir. There were several members besides the ushers wearing the gold shirts sprinkled sporadically throughout the church.

Several people poured into the church. The youth outnumbered the adults. He didn't see Star upon entering, but he knew she was there. He hadn't gotten up early, showered and gotten dressed. He constantly checked her location and when he noticed Star was at church, he let Kavon know it was time for them to leave.

The Young and the Reckless

Kavon followed him to the third pew from the front of the church. As they walked down the aisle Kavon kept turning to look back. He didn't understand why they had passed up so many pews before they took a seat. Cinque wanted to make sure Star seen him. He headed straight to the front of the church. When the usher told him to sit anywhere, he like, he knew there were no seating arrangements.

One of the youths in the church made their weekly church announcements, then the other church members took up tithes and offerings and the pastor lead them into prayer. The pastor then asked for all the visitors to stand. Cinque stood up. When it was his turn to make an announcement, he gave his name along with Kavon's name. He knew Kavon was not about stand up nor introduced himself. He was only there in support of him. This was Kavon's first time attending a church service. He had been inside several churches, but each visit was to pay his respects for a deceased friend or family member. As Cinque finished introducing, he and Kavon to the church, he let the entire congregation know he was a friend of Star. A few praise God and several amen echoed through the church.

Star was sitting on the first pew in the church. When the guest was instructed to stand, she turned to take a glance of the congregation. Her stomach instantly began to be overwhelmed with the butterfly feeling. She smiled when she noticed Cinque and his friend. He was sitting to the left of her in a separate section. Star and Cinque had a perfect view of one another from where they were seated.

Kavon looked over at his friend and became amazed. He had never seen Cinque blush. Kavon had seen him laughed at jokes and cry when he was mad. The look he was displaying while in this church was a first for Kavon. He had seen Cinque interact with all kinds of girls. He had never seen Cinque display this type of demeanor before. Serenity had his time, but he realized Star must have had his heart. Watching Cinque as he gazed in Star's direction made him realized that his friend was in love.

Star was a very active member of Mt. Pleasant. Her grandmother had been taking her to Mt. Pleasant ever since she was born. Cinque had visited the church a few times with his parents when he was younger. Star's grandmother would often invite them to different church functions. They always attended during Mt. Pleasants church anniversary.

Star smiled looking Cinque over from head to toe. To her he looked stellar. Even though he had on some Jordan's they complemented the tailored black suit he was wearing. She noticed his friend didn't look to bad either. Kavon had dressed up his distressed black denim with a Ralph Laruen Black Label dress jacket. They both appeared to be some distinguished young men. Star thought to herself, they clean up will.

Star's friend Davida had sent her the screenshot of Cinque laying shirtless in the breast of an unknown female. Star felt as though this had to be something serious because in her eyes Cinque looked very relaxed in the arms of another female.

The Young and the Reckless

Although she and Cinque had just reconnected that hadn't made anything official, she felt as though she was something special to him. He hadn't shown her anything different. She hated sending him to voicemail every time he called but she had no other choice. That picture had her in her feelings. She didn't want to have to compete with anyone. She felt as though if they were meant to be it would be.

The Pastor called Star's name to come up to the altar. Star gracefully walked up to the church altar and Deacon Brown an older gentleman that would put you in the mind of Ice Cube when you looked at him grabbed her by the hand. He assisted her up the steps.

Star looked out into the congregation. Her grandmother sat with the other five mothers of the church. She was wearing a grin with her plump figure and silver hair. Star's grandmother sat with mere confidence as she gave Star the head nod for approval.

Star opened with the usual church opening, giving thanks to God along with the pastor, assistant pastor, deacons etc. Along with her opening, she announced the three bible verses which inspired her sermon. She took a deep breath and began to preach her sermon.

Sometimes I along with countless others find it hard serving the Lord as a young individual. A few that we surround ourselves with and even those out in this vicious world assumes that if we change, we will lose who we are, especially when you're around my age. The truth of the matter is with this whole changing ordeal, if we change for Christ, we find who we are.

The congregation applauded. There were people screaming out preach girl. A few amen could be heard amongst the crowd.

Deuteronomy 3:6 says "be strong and courageous. Do not be afraid or terrified because of them, the Lord your God goes with you; he will never leave you nor forsake you." That's one of the reasons you can feel like the man when you walk through.

Star paused and glanced to see if they were all on the same page. The young individuals smile and chuckled as they could relate to the Rich Homie Quan song *Walk Thru* that Star was referring to in her sermon. She waited until they had settled down before she continued.

We all have a purpose in this world. It doesn't matter who you are, you need to know that you have a purpose. It's up to you to take time and discover your purpose. If you feel like you are losing instead of winning, go to the mirror and have a talk with your number one team player. When you get that little feeling down on the inside. Like the one I just got right before I came up here, you know that something types of feeling that gives you the urge, that's God letting you know its time to let that team know its time for a change. We are all in the will of God. We are alive to fulfill his purpose not ours. Jeremiah 29:1 tells us "For I know the plans I have for you, declares the Lord, plans to prosper you and not to harm you, plans to give you and a future." Our

The Young and the Reckless

purpose is to not be heartless are doing the unthinkable like letting several people make our beds rock. See the difference between me and you I rather severe the Lord. I don't never have worry about being broke or broken. I'm not interested in being knocked down like dominoes and feeling some type of way afterwards.

The congregation applauded. Star tried to discreetly lick her lips and took sip of water for the first time from the glass that was sitting near the podium Often people go to church and hear the pastor preach and while listening to the words that rolls off the tongue of the pastor people get the feeling that those words are directed towards them. Cinque knew she was talking to him. He was holding on to every word. Star hands was strategically placed on the podium. She was very articulate as she spoke. She didn't move about as most pastors. Her delivery was more like Michelle Obama's when she spoke of going high when they go low. She stood with elegance and pride as she read from her notes.

There are plenty things that attract us to sin. The Loud can sometimes call us up personally. The glitter and the gold will have some of the prettiest people doing the ugliest things. The flesh does get weak. Try to go a week without HIM and see just how weak you will be. The enemy can form a weapon that may begin to manifest. But we already know that weapon will not prosper. HE told us. There's a flip side of that though, everybody is not your enemy, and some people are silently working in your favor. So, as we go Outside Today and any other day, we must stop falling in the traps that are set before us. We must stop being satisfied with the mediocre. Just know living without God is just like trying to dribble a football. Amen.

The congregation let out woes of Amen as they applauded. Kavon looked over toward his friend. He could see the admiration gloating upon his face as he didn't blink as his eyes were glued upon Star.

Knowing that God has a process that we will have to go through. HE may continue to have us go through this process until we get it right. However, we cannot afford to be side tracked nor distracted by the glitter and gold ore every female or male friend we encounter. But we have gotten too busy for God. No one wants to take the time out of their day to go through the process. Amen.

Those amongst us even those day ones can sometimes detour us from the real assignment that God intends us to go through. We can't ignore the road blocks because there will be some struggles with our name on it. God appoints us all to our trials and tribulations. Oh yeah, it's not uncommon for HIM to try you.

As I come to an end, I want to remind you that Romans 12: -2 tells us that, "1 Therefore, I urge you, brothers and sisters, in view of God's mercy, to offer your bodies as living sacrifice, holy and pleasing to God-this your true and popper worship. 2 Do not conform to the pattern of this world but be transformed by the renewing of your mind. Then you

The Young and the Reckless

will be able to test and approve what God will is his good, pleasing and perfect will."

As I go, know that Christ will shine upon you. No longer will you have to focus on the past or be concerned with anything that the naysayers have said or will say. As long as you and God know, HE's all you have to answer to. Young people, it's time to live according to HIS will. Be federal for HIM. As I close, I just want to ask all my peers, is anybody ready for change.

The entire church stood their feet. There were tears following and a lot of shouting going on. The pastor embraced Star and mouthed great job. He then took over the mic.

"We have to change with purpose!" the pastor yelled like Pastor Basie on the TV show Greenleaf. He continued to bellow, "Turn to your neighbor. Say neighbor, I've been redeemed." There was not a head amongst the congregation who hadn't turned. The choir who had been sitting behind the pulpit hadn't uttered a word. They now were standing and singing LaShun Pace's *I Know I've Been Changed*. When the song was over the pastor open the doors of the church. A few had joined. Some were old, and some were young.

Cinque waited until things look to be over. He was going to approach Star before she got out of his view. He was headed in her direction.

"You almost had me about to join." Cinque told Star.

"Why didn't you?" she asked.

He wasn't expecting that comeback. Although, he heard what she preached, and it made sense to him. He knew it was time for him to make a change. He had been skipping out on basketball practices. He had even missed the districts that had taken place. He had been ignoring his coach phone calls and he couldn't say why.

Cinque took the focus off him, "Star, that was awesome."

"Yeah, you were over here stepping all on our toes." Kavon chuckled, "I'mma keep knocking these hoes down like dominoes though."

Cinque tapped Kavon on the shoulder, "Dude, chill out. We are in a church." He looked around the church. He noticed that a few members who were wearing the gold oxford shorts were looking in their direction. "Star, what are your bout to get into?" he thought to himself that didn't come out right. He prayed that she didn't let anything slick roll off her tongue to imply or insinuate that he would be get into her.

Star let him know that she would call him later on after she had gotten her grandmother settled in at home. She even let him know she was done ignoring his calls. Cinque took her into his arms and embraced her tightly. They say their goodbyes. He and Kavon made their exit as the rest of the congregation congregated.

The Young and the Reckless

CHAPTER 14

Neveah made her way up to the 7th floor of Queenly Tower at Barnes-Jewish Hospital. She stepped of the elevator and proceed towards Paradise's room. In just five days Paradise was back to normal. She only had a few skin abrasions on her face and arm. There was nothing about her that said she was thrown from the car.

"Whoever is praying for me, I don't need them to stop." Neveah overheard Paradise say as she entered her hospital room. Paradise said a few more things to the caller before she ended the call as she embraced Neveah with a warm hug, she greeted her with as she leaned into the hospital bed in which Paradise occupied.

"Did you see Rome when you were headed this way?" Paradise asked.

"He out?" Neveah inquired.

"He got out the same day. The only held him for a few hours." Paradise stated.

"Who praying for that fool? You mean to tell me dude get caught in stolen car, killed the person he crashed into and they didn't hold him for twenty-four hours. Let me call my brother." Neveah pulled her cellphone out of the pocket of the True Religion jeans she was wearing. She went to his name and pressed on it. She put the phone up to her ear and listened to the phone rang. "Que." She didn't give him time to respond, "You know Rome out of jail already."

He responded, "Yeah. I know but they just issued another warrant out for his arrest. It was a strap found in that truck. The way it sounds that strap has a few bodies on it. That reminds me. I need to call your uncle back. Serenity told me about some dudes that tried to do a home invasion. Well, they did but they didn't get nothing. She says dude had a cardinal bird tatted on his hand."

"Don't that dude Kevin that runs one of uncle's spot has a red cardinal bird tattoo or hangs out with someone that does?" Neveah waited for her brother to respond. He confirmed it and she let him know she was up at the hospital with Paradise. Shortly the call came to an end.

Neveah turned to Paradise, "I think Rome bout to go back to jail. They found a gun in that truck he stole, and it has some murders on it."

Paradise gave Neveah a strange look, "Remember a truck like the one we were in Chicago? They crashed into the people that were behind us."

Neveah looked in Paradise direction as she took a seat on her hospital bed. She began to speak, "Vaguely. I know it's probably a coincidence though that a truck you had an accident in almost hit us."

The Young and the Reckless

"I don't know. The truck was bent on the front bumper and the passenger side had a few scratches like it had been in an accident." Paradise warned.

"I don't think Rome killed anybody. He doesn't even have the guts to car jack people like this crazy people out here doing." Neveah spoke in Rome's defense.

"Now he will bust a window and use a screwdriver to take someone's parked car while they are not watching." Paradise confirmed Rome was a car thief. He just took cars from their owners when the car was unoccupied.

Neveah's cell phone began to ring. She didn't recognize the number that was flashing across the screen. "Hello." The annoyance of the phone call could be heard in her voice.

"Neveah?" Serenity was trying to make sure the right person was on the phone. She retrieved the number from Cinque's phone. She knew that the contact name 'LIL SIS' had to be his sister Neveah, but the way she answered the phone she wasn't sure.

"This is Neveah. Who is this?"

"Neveah, this is Serenity. I got your number from your brother Cinque.

Neveah knew Cinque hadn't gave out her number. He would have at least told her, but she knew who Serenity was to her brother. He had mentioned her a few times, but she didn't feel it was too serious. He had never taken the time out to make sure he introduced her to anyone. She was willing to listen to whatever Serenity to have to say.

While Neveah was on the phone, Paradise decided to give Rome a call. His phone would ring once and then the voicemail would pick up. After the fifth time she dialed the number someone answered and then hung up. She dialed the number again and it went straight to his voicemail.

Paradise instantly became concerned. That was unlike him to ignore her call. In the pit of her stomach she could feel something wrong. She looked to Neveah and she had a confused look upon her face as she held her cellphone up to her ear. Paradise waited patiently for Neveah to end her call. She became anxious to find out who Neveah had been listening to for almost five minutes. She needed to tell her friend what had just happened as she call Rome. She needed someone to help her make sense out of call that she wouldn't know what was going on the other end of the line she was calling.

Five minutes turned to ten minutes. She watched Neveah as she walked back and forth in her hospital room. Whoever Neveah was listening to had her undivided attention. Neveah was engaged in conversation where she hadn't said a word. Neveah sat down on Paradise's hospital bed and tears began to slowly creep down her face. She leaned into Paradise and she could do was hold her friend. She was trying her best to comfort her. Paradise didn't know what to say or what to do. When Neveah ended the call, Paradise immediately bawled, "Who we gotta kill?" she didn't know why

The Young and the Reckless

they were crying. She was going to wait to see what Neveah had to say.

CHAPTER 15

Spring break had slithered in slowly but ended abruptly. So much had took place in the ten days they were away from school. Cinque had enjoyed all the support he had on decision day. He was so focused on decision day that it took his focus off his Prom. Star hadn't asked him about prom, so he didn't bother asking her. He could remember getting ready for the cotillion his church was having one year. He mother told him the next time he would probably wear a tuxedo would be to his prom. She had carried on about how she couldn't wait for the day. It saddens him that neither she or his dad was there to witness him going to prom. He put all his thoughts on his decision day. Sports was more of Pharaoh and his parents were all about academics. He was honored to make his uncle proud of him. Pharaoh bragged so much on his nephew talents all kind of people that his uncle knew was looking out to hear about where he was deciding to attend college.

Cinque decision day picture along with him and Coach Porter had gone viral. It was as though the entire high school and the college basketball team had shared the photo and it hadn't stopped being shared once it hit social media.

The Young and the Reckless

Cinque was representing the college of his choice which was located in West Lafayette, Indiana to the fullest. A university in Las Vegas was trying to intrigue him with many perks. Even though students are not allowed to be paid, they were gifting him things from apple watches, shoes from Nike, Adidas and Puma; video games and they had given Pharaoh all types of appliances. Pharaoh loved the Keurig and the year supply of various k-cups. As much as Pharaoh enjoyed the gifts, he left it up to his nephew to make the final decision. Cinque wanted to be close to home and his next choice had too much racial tension. Students were protesting due the injustices it was undergoing.

Brittany, Pharaoh's beauty of the month, helped him with his college decision. It wasn't so much that she helped but the conversation prior to his visit to the college let him know he was making the best choice. Besides, his Coach let him know he wouldn't ride the bench his freshman year. The other two colleges pretty much had their star players. He would be amongst the top three players with the college in Indiana. They also offered the major he was most interested. He would be a double major in Business Marketing and Graphic Design. He had a strong interest in the Robotics program. He learned how to use computer software to design new images and functions for the robots. The month before his parent's gruesome death had one an award in a regional competition. He was recognized for designing, building and programming a robot. He exemplified overall excellence in creating a high-quality robot. Most people didn't know that because that desire took a backseat. Tragedy struck and had stolen his passion, along with the morals and values that had been bestowed upon him by his parents.

    Brittany came in one weekend to visit his uncle in March and hadn't left. While she was here, she found out that her son's paternal grandparents were seeking custody of her only son. She didn't understand because she allowed them to keep him during the school year. They also had alternate holidays. She had been kind of enough to sign documents to grant the guardianship being that she wasn't in town. She didn't want them to come across any complications with medical issues should any had occurred. She came across an announcement in the *St. Louis American*. Brittany had picked up the well-known local paper when she left out of Schnucks grocery store. She always found the *PARTYLINE* quite interesting. A journalist highlighted the weekly events that took place throughout the city. Brittany compared the journalist who wrote the column to Wendy Williams and Gary with the Tea. She spilled the tea and gave her point of view on the happenings in the STL.

    Had she not been in St. Louis there was no way she would have not seen the announcement. The newspaper was popular in St. Louis and although they had the paper online, she didn't even think about viewing the online version. The newspaper had been around over eight-five years and to her St. Louis was the only paper it had gain popularity. It was no way she would have seen it Phoenix. They were petitioning the court for full custody. She had to present at every hearing. She found that she had missed six court appearances.

The Young and the Reckless

Things were not working in her favor. She appeared to be the negligent parent they made her out to be. She was about to lose legal custody of her minor seven-year-old child.

Together, Brittany and Cinque were both filling voids. Even though Cinque was much older than her son, he had converted to the ten-year-old. She was giving Cinque the family nucleus he once had that someone highjacked him of when he was ten years old. Today, she was about to take him to the mall and help him pick out the perfect outfit for his graduation and his graduation party.

Cinque had convinced Brittany to take him to Frontenac Plaza. Frontenac was considered to be leading luxury mall in the St. Louis area. High end stores like Louis Vuitton were located there. Cinque was interested in going to Neiman Marcus. He was more t-shirt, jeans and jogging suit individual. He and his crew would go the area Footlockers to purchase a few items every now and again. His sister Neveah would pick him up things like Lacoste, Rock Revivals or any fashions that were on the scene. Of course, he paid for it, but she loved shopping, so he just let his little sister who could be found in the mall every weekend take care of that of his life.

Cinque had hung out with Brittany for a few hours longer than expected. She told him she wanted to stop by and see if her son was outside. Brittany's son grandparents stayed on the same street as Serenity. Cinque couldn't believe the coincidence. He hadn't spoken with Serenity since their little rendezvous. He had blocked her from calling his cellphone. When he saw her speaking with her neighbor, he thought about the home invasion she had experienced. He never spoke to his uncle about the incident. Seeing her reminded him of the conversation he needed to have with Pharaoh. He was glad that he was not in his car. He didn't want Serenity to think he was spying on her. Little did he know she thought that anyway. The legal tint prevented her from making eye contact. She knew that was Pharaoh's silver Benz. Serenity eyes moved along as the car rode by. It was as though she had made eye contact with Cinque through the tint. She watched until she could know longer see the car.

    Cinque, Demond and Kavon were now high school graduates. Everyone was there in support of the graduates. Cinque had received so many accolades. His family was there to cheer him on. His grandparents, his sister and his uncle along with Brittany and Paradise were amongst his supporters. Cinque didn't call Serenity about the graduation. He had already had plans for the night. He and Star graduated on the same day just a few hours apart.

    Cinque and Star had reconciled without mentioning the fact of what happened which led her to avoiding him. Being that their graduation had a minor inconvenience, they made plans to hang out together afterwards. Cinque was proud his family was there to support him throughout all his endeavors. They showed up at all his basketball games and any other major ceremony he partook in.

    The crew made it to their destination. They were being seated and Cinque looked around in

The Young and the Reckless

amazement. He was glad they were there but Star being there was the highlight of his evening. He was even glad to have Paradise there to support him. He knew her accident could had gone a lot different. He had received his high school diploma and was ready for his party. His uncle had reserved and area at the Marquee. Marquee was a Restaurant & Lounge near downtown St. Louis. Pharaoh lounges were on a smaller scale. Most preferred to his lounges as hole in the walls. His hole in the walls generated a lot of cash follow. He was tucked in neighbor hoods and it gave people places to go without going far. He wanted to check this venture out so what better excuse to go there and scout. Brittany was the one that told him he needed to pursue a larger scale in the nightclub scene and he was considering it.

Cinque rocked his all white Ralph Lauren with his white Giuseppe Zanotti shoes. His black Salvatore Ferragamo belt with the silver logo buckle was the only items he wore that were not white. Cinque looked like he had stepped off the set of Trevor Jackson's movie *Superfly* as one of the drug dealer villains in Snow Patrol. He stood out amongst his family and friends. He was the only one in all white. Cinque was afraid to eat. He didn't want to get any of his white dirty. Brittany told him to take his shirt off and he did.

They were partying amongst the party goers. Demond was about to hit the stage and perform one of the songs he had been working on in the studio. Right has one of the owners of the Marquee called Demond to the stage he walked passed Serenity as he saw her standing in the door looking around. She had to be wearing a fitted tee because the bulge in her stomach he had never noticed before. He didn't know what to do. He was definitely stuck in between warning his friend and performing. He pulled out his phone and prayed that Cinque would see the warning. He did. He stayed in his section and would watch his friend's performance from where he was. Neveah's radar was on and ready. She saw Serenity before she saw her. She led Paradise to the dance floor. Cinque watched as his sister went to take care of this situation. He couldn't believe what he was seeing. Amongst the crowd was a pregnant individual that he had sexual relations on many occasions with no protection.

Neveah and Paradise met Serenity at the door where she stood still surveying the club looking for her suspect as though she was a detective on the First 48. Neveah grabbed Serenity by the hand and led her to the stage. She whispered in Serenity's ear that Que was near the stage with his friend. Demond began to perform. The crowd was a tad bit uninterested. The moment he said, "I can tell she from St. Louis from the way she arches her back." The crowd went wild, and he now had their full attention. Kavon let Cinque know he was about to get closer to the stage. Cinque let he know he was about to leave. They dapped each other up and Kavon moved closer the area of the stage. Cinque moved passed Brittany, so he could be in ear reach of Pharaoh. He leaned into his uncle as he sat smiling bobbing his head to the dope beat Demond had created himself. Cinque whispered in his Pharaoh's ear and let him know that he and Star was about to leave. He didn't go into detail, but he let Pharaoh know that Serenity was there.

    Star was ready to go after the first twenty minutes of being at the club. Her conscious began to bother her. The music didn't so much bother her. She listened to a few of the mumble rappers, but it was the dancing just about all the females in the club were displaying. They were not partaking in a regular two-step. The girls were literally having a twerk off. She felt as though she couldn't be preaching about growing a relationship with God and her actions displayed different. She knew Cinque was celebrating and she didn't want to appear to be the party pooper.

    Cinque and Star made their exit. Serenity didn't see them make their escape. Cinque got in his car with Star in tow. As soon as he placed the key in the ignition and turned it, his gas light flashed warning him he was low on gas. He and Star were headed to the gas station. He stopped at the BP which was located on Natural Bridge and Grand Avenue. He got out and went to pay for his gas. Star scrolled in her phone as he pumped the gas. Cinque seen at least three faces walking back to their car coming from Popeye's chicken across the street from the gas station. He was praying that Latrell's homeboys hadn't seen him. Cinque had paid for forty dollars' worth of gas and the pump was only at nineteen. He figured he would just have to get gas elsewhere. He hung the pump up and hopped in the car. He watched the three males every move. He waited to pull off and they were doing the same thing. He decided to take the chance and leave thinking that they had not seen him. He stopped at the edge of the lot as they were at the edge of Popeye's lot. He made at right turn and so did they. He made it to the red light and kept going. The three males were in high pursuit. Star had looked up from her phone when she noticed his was driving too fast.

    Cinque noticed an individual sitting in the window of the passenger side of the car. When he saw the gun, he drove faster. The back window shattered. Star began to scream, and he scram through traffic. The males were on their target. Cinque informed Star they were going to have to get out the car. Cinque had almost lost control of the car. One of the bullets had struck the tire and Cinque couldn't get control of the car. He turned the corner and crashed into a brick house that sat on the corner. The males were nowhere in sight. Cinque led Star down the alley. He held her hand as he pulled her long the way. She hadn't panicked but fear had her moving at top speed. They cut through someone's backyard and made it the next block. Cinque peeked from the side of the house to make sure no one was coming down the street. He desperately tried not to look back at Star. He wanted to assure her that they would be okay, but he wasn't so sure. He had heard countless times if you need to take a gun where you go, you don't need to be there. He had kept his gun in his car's stash box and one run in with the police had him remove it. He wasn't yet old enough to be licensed to carry. He thought about Philando Castile. He was pulled over while driving in Falcon Heights, Minnesota. He was licensed to carry but still lost his life. Cinque had several thoughts about being caught with that gun.

The Young and the Reckless

He played out several scenarios. Each scenario led to him believing removing the gun from the car was the best choice. He currently felt a little different being that he was being gun down. He just wanted the dudes off him.

Cinque believed he didn't have a known car. It was typical of a single woman to have the same type of car. He thought about how he must have stood out. All white and looking Godly had caught the wrong attention.

It was a Thursday May night. It felt like mid-spring, but no one was out in the city. This was more than unusual. Warm nights the city streets were usually field. He and Star made it to the next block down an alley and found a garage to hid. Star looked at Cinque and took a deep breath. She was relieved that were safe for the moment. She said a little prayer and she didn't quite understand that being filled with a lot of adrenaline overcame the fear she thought she would have. She could her cars skidding through the area. Star watched Cinque as he called his uncle.

Torrance had just made it to the club to come celebrate. Pharaoh told Brittany what was going on and let her know she was going to have to catch a ride with Neveah. Pharaoh let Torrance know what Cinque had just phoned him. Torrance became outraged when heard the part about him bailing from the car. Demond had just came off stage from competing his performance that had the whole crowd yelling he from the Lou.

Cinque dropped his location. Pharaoh was leading the way to go rescue his nephew. Cinque could hear the car speeding down the blocks. His uncle with his goons showed up like Johnnie on the spot.

Once in the car with his uncle, he walked him through what had happened. They rolled passed his car and it was engulfed in flames. Latrell's homeboys had set the car on fire. They couldn't catch him so that took their anger out on his car.

Star was a nervous wreck. While they waited on Pharaoh tears began to roll down her face. She didn't make a sound, but she prayed. She was praying for her and Cinque. Before she ended her silent prayer, Pharaoh was pulling up to rescue to them.

Pharaoh took Star and Cinque to his home. Torrance, Kavon, and Demond were right behind them. Pharaoh didn't want Star to go home. He didn't know if she had friends that she would share the events of the night with, so he was trying to control that. He had some phone calls to make and people to see. He needed footage from the cameras that was in that area and he was going to get it.

For a brief moment Star was scared. She had gone through life having faith in her Lord and Savior. This moment she somehow only found faith in Que. When she looked at him, she saw someone that was calm under pressure. She believes he only ran because he was trying to protect her and get her out the line of fire. She could tell he didn't have a gun. She knew it must have been one in his car before

The Young and the Reckless

because he reached to grab it and hit the dashboard once he realized it wasn't there. She found comfort in being under Cinque. She didn't know if he was scared. He didn't have fear on his face. What she was rage. He was busy trying to comfort her and let her know that they were safe and everything would be okay. She believed him when he told her that she was safe. That feeling she had on this night was the end to nothing but the beginning of everything for Cinque and Star.

CHAPTER 16

Patty was pacing back and forth in the kitchen. Her mother ate her dinner and watched as the rear of Patty's feet lifted from the kitchen floor repeatedly. The television was on, but no one was attuned to the broadcast which was being displayed. Patty walked at a steady speed without no particular destination. Her faced expressed anxiety and annoyance. She had dialed Star's cellphone number to no avail.

Pharaoh had convinced Star that she needed some rest and relaxation. He let her know that he was going to send her and Cinque to The Ritz-Carlton. This was a luxury hotel with elegant dining and a full-service spa. It was list at the top ten best Saint Louis luxury hotel. She agreed but she let him know she need to stop by her place and pick up some personal items. Plus, she had to check on her grandmother and mother. She had left her phone in Cinque's car and hadn't spoken with her family all evening. They didn't quite understand why she wouldn't be celebrating her graduation with her own family. They eventually agreed to let her go and made plans to celebrate with at a later date.

Pharaoh wanted Cinque to keep an eye on Star. He knew Patty's close friend worked for SLPD. He didn't want Star saying anything about what had taken place. He gave Cinque specific instructions on

The Young and the Reckless

taking Star home and returning so he could drop them off at the Ritz-Carlton

Star knocked on the door and Patty ran towards the door. Star had texted Patty to let her know that someone was shooting at them before she had left her phone in the car. Patty assumed that word had gotten out that she was going to testify in a murder case and some was gunning her daughter seeking revenge. Patty decided that she was not about to testify, and she was not about to call her friend. She wouldn't know what to do if her daughter lost her life behind any decisions she had made.

Cinque parked and followed Star in her home as instructed. She didn't want him to sit in the car while she went in the house. She thought she was going to have to tell him to come in the house with her. When she noticed he was right behind her she felt a sense of comfort and protection she had just felt. Star let her mother and grandmother know that they she was going to hangout with Cinque. Her grandmother gave her approval. She had planted in Star her entire life her three rules to success. Her first rule was to graduate high school. The second rule was getting a good job or go to college. The third rule was wait until the age of twenty-three to get married and then have babies. She knew she had preached her rules enough Star lived by her rules of success. If she was going to go against those rules, she would do it with extreme precautions.

Cinque was headed back to meet his uncle. When he pulled in the garage Neveah was waiting on him. She had to let him know about all the things Serenity had told her about. Serenity was ready to apply some pressure and Neveah didn't know how long she was going to be able to babysit her with the lies she was using to keep her off her brother. When she saw Star, she knew it was going to have to wait.

Cinque wasn't in house a good five minutes. He grabbed what he thought he needed and headed back out of the door. Star followed Cinque over to guest registration. She looked around the corridor. Tall columns aligned the walkway, uplifting the salmon colored ceiling. A three-tier fountained graced the center of the corridor. There were vases of peach roses placed upon decorative console table in the hallway. Star was quite impressed by the entrance. She couldn't wait to see what the room had instore.

Star and Cinque reached their hotel suite. Cinque opened the door and motioned his head to let Star know to go ahead in the room. Star stopped in her tracks. She looked around the room and was quite impressed by what she was witnessing. She had never experienced such luxury. The elegant design transcending a modern look of sophistication. She had stepped foot in a Presidential Suite that had a spacious, two-story layout. There was a spiral staircase connecting the living area and bedroom. The large picture window displayed the city's skyline. She wanted to ask how much it cost and how long were they going to be there. She didn't.

The Young and the Reckless

Cinque admired Star's admiration of the room. His uncle had exposed him and his sister to these luxuries every time they took a family trip. The only thing different about this experience was he had plans on christening every section of the suite if Star was willing and ready.

Star was about to take a shower. The dirt and grit from the night couldn't be seen but she felt it. Cinque had showered and taken off his all white gear that became filthy as they ran through the streets of St. Louis to escape the shooters that were trying to end his life. Star was surprised her mother or grandmother didn't mention him being so dirty. They probably never looked him over. Patty was just concerned with seeing her daughter alive.

"Que, I want to make some things clear. You are not about to smash. I hope you know that I am saving myself for my future husband. I'm not about to put any miles on this her engine." Star patted her vagina as she let Cinque know where she stood about sex.

Cinque knew it wasn't about to go down. She crushed his christening every section of the hotel suite dreams. She had addressed him by Que. She had his undivided attention. As bad as he wanted to get up and between her, he respected her wishes.

Star had showered and as soon as she placed her head on the pillow she was out for the night. She was getting the rest she needed. She had an eventful night. The night seemed very impractical to her, but it happened. She had reconnected with someone she idolized. She knew he didn't live the perfect life, but he was captivating to her. It was her spirit to love all, only trust a few and do wrong to none. She felt that enough wrong had been done to him and she wasn't going to just walk away from him. She just wanted him to know she knew she wasn't the only one he was into. She'd just wanted to make it clear that she be the only one he wasn't getting into.

Cinque grinned as he admired the birthmark, she often hid with a baseball cap. She had showered and pulled her back into a ponytail. He knew Star was not in a rush to commit to doing him or being with him. She was trying to establish and improve what existed amongst them. He knew she had morals and even though they didn't address the picture with Serenity, he knew it bothered her something terrible. He knew in Star he had someone that would dedicate their time, energy and thoughts on a quest that would be inspired by kindness and compassion.

Cinque had put Serenity on the backburner. He hadn't so much called her or asked his uncle about the people who participated in invading her home. Now he was trying to figure out what type of father he would be and how accepting Star would be with the situation. He wasn't ready to lose touch with her again. Some how he had been taught that love can co-exist with pain and abuse. He was gone to have to let Serenity to know that she had set herself up for a disappointment, but they would have to come to a compromise. Star was his soulmate. He was not about to let nothing, or no one come in between that.

The Young and the Reckless

CHAPTER 17

Pharaoh decided that it was time for he and Brittany to spend some quality time together. They both had a lot on their mind. The issues that they were both facing was causing a bit of tension. When the sun had rose and begin peaking into his bedroom he decided to go ahead and a rise as well. He stood up and noticed that Brittany was still asleep. He wanted to wake her and let her know that he had made plans for her to be pampered. Often times when he had gotten up, she would open her eyes. As he placed his hand on the door knob of his bedroom door, he stopped and turned back to grab his cellphone as it vibrated on the nightstand. He jogged over to the nightstand trying not to wake Brittany. He missed the call from his mother. He immediately called her back.

"Ma," he said once he heard her voice, "you hung up as soon as I had grabbed my phone. Is everything okay. You usually don't call me this early." He waited on her response.

"No. Everything is not okay. I am here at the hospital with your father. He kept telling me that he was dizzy and once he fell, I knew it was best that we go and find out what's going on with him. Right now, they are running and test. I was going to wait to call you until we found out what was going on, but the doctor told me to call me family, so I wouldn't be here alone."

Pharaoh ended the call with his mother after he found out what hospital his parents were. He headed to the shower to freshen up and make his away to check on his parents. He let Brittany know where he was going. She insisted that she was about to go with him. He tried to tell her about the appointment he made with the spa and Tia so that she could get some royal treatment. She let him know that she appreciated it but being there for him was more important to her.

When he and Brittany made it to the hospital something had come over him. The feeling he was experiencing he had felt it before. He couldn't move from the seat of the car. Brittany was in her phone, so she wasn't paying him any attention. He took a deep breath. The butterflies grew, and he had a strange feeling as though there were a million butterflies in his stomach just crashing into on another. He tried to move again, and he felt as though someone had placed a boulder in his lap. He became weary and weak. He closed his eyes and when he opened them back up, he was able to gather himself. He grabbed the door handle to his freedom. The weight had been lifted. Brittany followed suit.

The door opens like magic as they entered the hospital. Together he and Brittany approached the information desk. He was trying to find out if his parents were still in the emergency room. The clerk let him know that he had moved him to fifth floor. He

The Young and the Reckless

and Brittany both thanked the man at the desk and headed to where he instructed them to go.

Dong. Was the sound heard before a voice spoke of the loud speaker. Ding. Was heard as the elevator doors open. People were hustling and bustling as though they were in downtown Manhattan, New York and the light had turned red. The walk across the street after the light turn red was like a race to the finish line when it came to getting across the street. You moved to slow people would walk over you, moving you right on out the way.

They made it to their floor and as soon as the doors opened, he seen his mother sitting in the waiting room. She was the epitome of style and grace. She sat neatly put together. Even with the pain in her eyes she was still beautiful. She was wearing the same look on her face when he went to comfort her when they hadn't gotten word about Xavier. He knew he had to be something really wrong with his dad. He and his dad didn't have the best father and son relationship, but that was his dad.

When she seen her son, she smiled with tears of joy creeping doing her face. She let him know that the doctor informed her to contact him once her family had arrived. She did just that. Pharaoh was not ready to hear that his father had stage four prostate cancer. They were given him four months to live. He hated to hear that, but he did not fret. He began to think about his mother. Who would keep her company? What would should do without his father? He had never seen them apart.

Teresa Seals

Pharaoh's father wasn't the most talkative individual, but he was the most supportive. Xavier Sr. showed up to every parent teacher's conference and the little league games he and his brother were involved in. He could remember his father telling he and his brother different stories about his childhood. He often reminded them that an evil spirt will cause you to mistreat people who could have been a blessing to you. He didn't quite understand the message then but today the reminder of the statement made him realize exactly what he meant. His father's diagnoses of prostate lead him into a prayer asking for patience, seeking peace and positivity.

Brittany didn't even know what to say. As a writer she couldn't muster up one word. Sitting in the waiting room of the hospital she stared at the décor and all she could see from the pink; blue and gray broken circles were images which she perceived has fungus that could be seen under any microscope. She walked over the vending machine and purchased a water. She attempted to checkout herself out in the glare of the vending machine glass. She smirked admiring her red and white Adidas track suit. Brittany had lost her usual flare of dressing up jeans with nice blouses and high heels since she had been around Pharaoh. He usually opted for track suits and jogging pants. She could see why. She felt so comfortable with her new attire. Classy casual lounge wear was what she considered it to coincide with.

Pharaoh decided to call his mother's sister, Alene. First, he asked his mother had she reached out to her. She let him know that he was the only

The Young and the Reckless

person who she had called. She told him to wait before he told Cinque and Neveah. He understood her reasoning. He only called Alene. She informed him she was on her way. His aunt was always around but she was only a phone call away. His aunt was the toting bible, only wore skirts type of woman. Alene could have had a starring role in *Eat Pray Love*.

Alene had made it to the hospital in no time. She was going to be there for the only family she had left. Pharaoh watched as two sisters talked never missing a beat. When the doctor entered the room, he let them know that they could visit with Xavier briefly. They were about to do a few short procedures that will help ease a small portion of his pain. Xavier had given his approval to the doctors to treat him.

Pharaoh checked in on his dad. He appeared to be in no pain, but his appearance had change. He was thinner man now than the stout one he had just seen last month.

After hours of being at the hospital, Pharaoh and Brittany left to grab a bite to eat. They both agreed on Chick-Fil-A. He and Brittany ate their food at the restaurant. Once they were done, they headed back to his house.

Brittany showered first and once she was done Pharaoh was walking in as if he was about to join her. She dried off and noticed a slight pug in her belly area. She was doing a lot more eating than exercise. She made a personal note that she was going to have to switch up the new regiment she had been subjected to ever since she started hanging around Pharaoh.

Brittany threw on a nightshirt she had picked up from Walmart. She grabbed the remote and started skimming through the channels. She was attempting to find her movie for her and Pharaoh to fall asleep to. She was not about to allow him to watch his favorite movie tonight. She was only going to give in if he suggested it. Brittany watched as he exited the bathroom wearing nothing but a smile.

"I've been told that birds do it. I've heard bees do it. When it's time to hit, I can make you weak in the knees." Pharaoh chuckled and continued with his rap, "I'm not a heavyweight like Money May Weather but I will definitely last a good twelve rounds. So, just relax cause I'm about to give you all that I got." Pharaoh climbed in the bed with Brittany.

She sneered and was flattered by his renewed energy. She decided to match his rap with, "I'm a buck fifty. I don't think you can hang. We not even in the same weight class."

Neveah was in the other room. She could hear a loud clapping and the furniture squeaking. She closed her door and put her headphones in and wondered of all nights why did she choose to be home alone.

Neveah needed some time to herself. For the first time in a long time she had no energy to rip and run the streets. She was so busy being there for everyone else she stopped being there for herself. It was time to refocus on her goals.

The Young and the Reckless

Neveah nuzzled her nose in some tissue. She then placed her hand by the nape of her neck. She felt as though she was about to come down with something. She went to the medicine cabinet and gulped down a dose of Nyquil. She wanted to call Demond but instead she called it a night.

CHAPTER 18

The summer sun was shining bright. The temperature had to have been in the mid 60's. That was odd for the summertime in St. Louis. The bipolar weather was not about to put a stop to what Neveah had planned for the day. Her only concern was making sure her hair and clothes were on point. She decided to take a trip to see Tia. She wasn't going to let anything interfere with her getting hair done.

Paradise decided to hang out with Neveah while she was headed to the beauty salon and whatever errands she was going to partake in. She had been cooped up long enough. Neveah was impressed by the progress Paradise made while recovering. You couldn't tell she was even in an accident that could have taking her life. She had a minor scar above her eyebrow. That scar could have easily been covered with some concealer if Paradise cared to hide the scar. For her it served as a reminder of just how blessed she was to have walked away from a near death experience and still be above ground to tell about it.

Tia took a brief glance at the door as Neveah and Paradise were buzzed into her establishment. She had recently had an electric door mechanism installed for security purposes. Torrance had been trying to get her to install some sort of security where

The Young and the Reckless

individuals didn't have easy accessibility to commit some sort of crime. She agreed because her safety was important to her. Tia looked up from the ponytail she was curling and greeted them both as they walked through the salon doors. Tia was finishing up on the client that was scheduled before Neveah. When Tia spun her chair around, so she could take a look at her hairstyle, Neveah couldn't believe her eyes. The long bouncy ponytail twirled, and Neveah had a clear view of Serenity's face.

Neveah tapped Paradise on the arm to get her attention, "Look at this!"

Paradise shook her head in disbelief before making a comment on the individual. "Fatal Attraction ass hoe!" Paradise chuckled while whispering when she responded to Neveah.

Neveah and Paradise didn't speak to Serenity. They took their respective seats in the salon and acted as though they didn't even notice her. Serenity wanted to make sure they'd acknowledge her presence. Serenity walked over to them. Standing directly in their face she spoke.

"Neveah, Tia does your hair too?" Serenity asked.

"Yes." Neveah was short. She had tagged Tia in all her pictures every time she styled her hair and she posted the picture to social media. Neveah knew that's how she found her anyway. She was not amused with her trying to act brand new about Tia being the one who styled her hair.

Tia observed the interaction. She walked over to them to inquire about the new individual whom hair she had just styled, "You all know each other?"

"Not really." Paradise interjected as she noticed Neveah was about to speak up.

Serenity turned towards Tia as she rubbed her belly. She began to speak, "This is my baby's aunt." She looked specifically at Neveah. Tia followed Serenity's eyes to see if she was speaking about Neveah because she knew nothing about Paradise having a brother that could make her an aunt.

Tia questioned with a look of discernment, "That's Que's baby?"

"Yes! It's his baby." Serenity said proudly.

The chatter of the salon that was taking place came to a halt. All eyes were on Serenity. The loud yes, she had spoken caught their attention. There were two other hairdressers and two barbers. For each worker they had approximately two clients each in the salon. No one really knew Que because he never came to the shop. They only knew of him and that's because Neveah had discussed having an older brother. Tia had a picture of him and Neveah at her station, along with other close friends. His only visit to the salon was when Tia first opened some time ago.

"Well okay." Tia replied trying to match Serenity's energy.

The Young and the Reckless

Serenity proudly bounced out of the hair salon after she made her announcement acknowledging Cinque as the father of her child. She exited the facility as though she was Kerry Washington portraying Olivia Pope walking with her white trench coat on down the corridors of the White House. Paradise stood up and imitated her after she exited. People chuckled as she imitated Serenity.

"Que gonna have some major problems with that crazy broad." Tia said as she escorted Neveah to the shampoo bowl.

Serenity was the topic of the salon's discussion after she pranced out of the door. Tia and Neveah talked about how Serenity had to see her tag her in all her post and took it upon herself to make an appointment with her. Serenity was working her way in to everyone's program that was affiliated with Cinque. Neveah had slipped up to tell her where the graduation party was being held. Serenity was talking and asking random questions. When she simply said I wonder what Que is doing after his graduation because she was trying to surprise him. Neveah didn't want her to make plans because he already had some. She mentioned his plans without even thinking about it. She didn't know her brother had moved on that fast. She didn't know how serious his relationship with Star was. She really didn't know much at all about her brother's relationships. He didn't bring anyone he dated around.

Neveah was in and out. Paradise convinced Neveah to take her to go see Rome while he was being held in St. Louis City jail. When they made it to the facility there were unable to see him. They didn't receive a valid reason, they were just told the visit was not going to take place. They turned and exited the facility the same way they came. Paradise didn't ask why. She wasn't familiar with the visiting process. She thought him being denied a visit was normal procedures.

Neveah and Paradise headed to the mall. Neveah was glad that her friend was still around to do the things they usually found themselves doing before the accident. One day when she was looking up some information on the internet, trying to see if they needed to be concerned with their case in Chicago and she came across a few tragic stories.

The first story she came across was about a girl by the name of Hadiya Pendleton. She was a 15-year-old Black girl from Chicago, Illinois, that was shot in the back and killed while standing with friends inside Harsh Park in Kenwood, Chicago after taking her final exams. Then there was another story about Kenneka Jenkins another young black female that was found dead in a walk-in freezer of a hotel in Chicago. She could only imagine how Hadiya and Kenneka friends and family had to feel. She was grateful she wasn't left to mourn Paradise.

Neveah said a silent prayer asking the Lord to grant anyone who is experiencing some sort of tragedy the strength to endure all misunderstandings in which they have encountered. She and Paradise had been through the best of times. She thanked God that she was still there with her to share a laugh. She couldn't find anything about her and Paradise's case. Neveah made a mental note about not going back to Chicago again. Chicago wouldn't be one of the places she chose for college or relocation. She was ready to leave St. Louis because of the same reason. Death lurked in the midst and around any corner. She had dealt with enough death in her short lifetime beginning with her mother and father. She was young at the time of their death but the pain of not having parents was unbearable.

There wasn't a lot of memories created with her parents. Although, she still remembered going to climb in their bed every night and her brother would come right after her. She missed that so much. She missed having mother and daughter moments. She thought about Brittany almost filling that void.

Neveah thought about the day when she and Brittany had officially bonded. One night she and Brittany were watching her uncle's favorite movie. Neveah found herself snugged on the couch right up under Brittany. Brittany was so accepting of the cuddle, she shared her blanket with her as she rested her feet on the ottoman in front of the couch. Pharaoh had come home that night and found them in the basement. He smiled admiring Brittany's beauty. She had impressed him on how she came in and started forming a relationship with his niece and nephew right off the bat. He had only brought three other females around them. They failed enormously. They were trying to get in his bed like they were going to put something on him and he'd move them in the next day. Those times of bringing women home were epic failures. He had reached the point in his life where he wanted to be loyal to his wife. He was tired of the games he played with the ladies. He no longer wanted to be sneaking and he surely didn't want to be considered cheating on any one. Looking at Brittany and Neveah bonding even while they were sleep appealed to him. He didn't even wake them the day he saw them sleeping on the sofa.

Before they went shopping, Neveah took Paradise to eat at a new restaurant she wanted to try out. After they had a burger and bottomless sweet potato fries from Red Robin and then they headed to the mall. Neveah had gotten her social security check and was about to blow it all at the mall. She was getting her an outfit to wear to court with Brittany. The judge was expected to rule in the case of her son Jarvis. Neveah thought it was no other way than to show her appreciation on how she stepped up and moved in practically becoming the mother she had be longing for since the death of her very own mother. Tia had been there for her for the longest of times, but she was more like a big sister. Her and Tia discussed things like sisters would do. She felt as comfortable with Tia and she did with Paradise. Brittany was different. She was saying and doing things quite different. She had some great advice. It made Neveah wonder how Brittany slipped up and lose custody of her only child.

As they were walking in the mall, Paradise pulled her phone from her fanny pack when she felt it vibrate. Paradise noticed she had received a text message from her doctor's office. It was a reminder of for her physical therapy appointment. She told her

The Young and the Reckless

friend about the reminder and asked Neveah to go with her. When she told Neveah the date, she almost turned her down because it was at the same day of Brittany's court date. She immediately sent Brittany a text message letting her know she would not be joining her in the morning with the reason along with it. Brittany let her know she understood and would be best to support her best friend. Neveah told Brittany to hold her head because bosses always come out on top. She knew being there for her friend was the best decision even though who she didn't quite understand why her friend who was back to her normal self still required physical therapy.

Neveah stayed the night with Paradise, so she wouldn't over sleep and be the reason she missed her doctor's appointment. She was not above pressing snooze. Being on time was one of her worst characteristics, but she was working on it. Brittany had even told her about why being time was important. Neveah listened but she always thought about time didn't wait on anyone so why should she.

Paradise and Neveah were about to grab a bite to eat from Taco Bell once they left the doctor's office. Neveah pulled up in front of her home. Paradise told her she needed to run home and check on her mother and grandmother before she went anywhere else. Her dad had become estranged and they all feared he might do something out of a jealous rage. He hadn't really been himself lately He would yell or scream a reply when someone asked a simple question. He only talked to Paradise in a calm tone. Neveah pulled up in front of her house. She got out the car and went inside her home. Neveah told Paradise to take her car and take her time. She left her self in through the garage and headed to the kitchen to sit down and eat her Taco Bell. Just as she pulled her items out the bag there was a knock on the door.

    Morning came, and court ended as fast as the day came. Brittany was distraught. Pharaoh was currently being her wingman as they poured out of the family court building. He didn't know what to say. He just placed his hand in the small of her back. Tears flowed sporadically as she was taking several deep breaths. She couldn't believe that the judge had granted Jarvis's paternal grandparents' full custody.

    They were out of the courthouse and in the parking lot about to enter Pharaoh's car. The sounds and the rupture of the car moving from Pharaoh trying to dodge potholes were the only things that could be heard with the muffles of Brittany's grief. Pharaoh stomach began growling screeched like DJ Khaled yelling *We the Best*! He was not use to leaving home and not eating breakfast. No one had to tell him breakfast was the best meal of they day.

    Pharaoh wanted to ask if she was hungry, but he decided against it. He just decided to drive to place where he could help his hunger pains. He felt the vibration from his Apple Watch. He pressed the button as he drove down Lindell Avenue headed to

The Young and the Reckless

the Central West End. Culpepper's sweet and tangy wings is what he had taste for since he was on that side of town. He figured Brittany could use a drink as well.

Pharaoh found parking right in front of the restaurant. In other time an individual would have to circle the block a few times to find parking. It was early though. He parked and walked over to the meter stand to pay for parking. Once he paid for parking, he walked back to the car to open Brittany's door and grabbed her hand, assisting her out the car. She wiped her face with her free hand and proceeded towards the door of Culpepper's. They seated themselves at the bar and placed their orders as soon as the bartender acknowledged them.

Pharaoh felt the vibration of his Apple Watch. He looked at and seen there was a message from Torrance. He pulled his phone out to get a closer look at the message.

I am trying to stay in my lane and ain't trying to beef with nobody. Body bags and toe tags, I must avoid.

Pharaoh chuckled at Torrance's text message. He knew exactly what that meant. He then sent Cinque a message and told him he would be to pick him up in the morning. His sweet and tangy wings along with the cheese steak fries were placed in front of him by the bartender. As he was about to take a bite his phone rang. He ignored because he didn't want to have to wipe his hand and pulls his phone out. He pressed the button on the watch and the call came through again. He just wanted to eat in peace, but Neveah was not about to let that happen.

He answered. She screamed, "Unk, where are you?"

"I'm five minutes from anywhere. What's up?"

"Some detectives just left and said they need to speak with you. The have a lead on the murderer who killed my mom and my dad." Neveah began to cry.

"I'm on my way." He turned to Brittany, "We have to go." Pharaoh stood up and pulled his money out of his pocket. He laid a hundred-dollar bill on the bar.

Brittany walked right out of Culpepper's with her glass in hand. She was not about leave her whole glass of Hennessy.

Once in the car, Pharaoh told Brittany to text Cinque and tell him change of plans. He was on his way now.

Moe Jackson and Kevin Terrell were plastered over each news channel network in the metropolitan area. Moe's face could be seen whereas the only thing that could be seen was the red Cardinal bird on Kevin's hand as he covered his face. Neither men were wearing handcuffs as they were escorted into Police Headquarters.

News anchors announced more about the suspects would be told on the five o'clock news. Pharaoh and retrieved his nephew and Star. He didn't know what to expect. Pharaoh start receiving

The Young and the Reckless

calls from people he hadn't heard from in years. Everyone was trying to see how he was doing or if he had found out about the individuals who had been captured in the murder of his family members. He wasn't trying to talk to anyone. All those people that was there when tragedy struck faded away and now, they had come back. He didn't want to be bothered with any of them. He was surrounded with the people he felt he needed to be around. He just knew he was about to go home and wait on the detectives to reach out to him again. He was going to be glued to the TV until he heard anything.

Cinque held his sister as she cried tears of joy and pain. Star watched as he embraced his younger sister. Pharaoh was one the phone with his mother. He was trying to answer as many of her questions as she could. He could barely make out what she was saying. She was muttering words and crying at the same time. As he ended the call with his mother there was a knock at the door. Pharaoh told Brittany to open the door assuming it was Torrance.

Paradise came running through the door, "I just got off the phone with Rome. He said they were trying to pin a murder to him because the weapon was found in the truck he had stolen. When they did ballistics on the gun it came up in a murder that happened when he was six years old. They were questioning him about the death of Xavier and Bria. One of the detectives looked at the dates. He is about to be processed and released." She said in all one breath. She hadn't seen the new or knew that they were already aware. She just knew that the car they were in the owner had to be involved with the death of her best friend's parents.

Chaos filled the air of Pharaoh's home. When the doorbell rang, he just opened the door. It was too late to close Serenity was in the door.

"You had them break into my house! You scan for that, Que!" Serenity with belly bulging was headed in Cinque's direction. She walked right passed Pharaoh as if he was there. She had words for Cinque. She couldn't get through on his phone, but he was about to hear all what she had say. When she saw the news and the hand of the two men who were in her home, she felt that Cinque had to be behind the home invasion.

CHAPTER 19

Demond pulled his phone from his pocket. He was about to give Neveah a call. They hadn't talked to each other in a few days and that was unusual for them. They hadn't spent much time together lately. It was as though he had put her in the friend zone. She was with Paradise creating a lifetime of memories while Demond was out grinding making a name for himself. He was getting paid to make club appearances and perform one of his songs. He was blowing up on YouTube from little snippets of freestyles he had done on his phone. He was now putting up his iPhone and getting a camera crew to take his journey to the next level. Demond was about to have a big day. He was scheduling to record his video right in his neighborhood for his most requested song *Can't Predict the Changes.*

The day had come in which he had been waiting for so long. All his hard work and dedication to his grind was getting noticed. Demond had made to the set early. He couldn't believe a big record executive had reached out to him. She wanted to see and hear a full-length song with video.

While he waited one of the neighborhood preachers stopped him and asked what he had going on out here. He said a few things to him. It was nothing out of the way and Demond wasn't disrespectful. Then the man flipped the script on him. He went from zero to a hundred quick. He was just giving him his props. Then he got confrontational. He was looking like David Banner. Well his appearance was more like what David Banner were to look like if he were homeless. His silver hair stood up on his head like a wild man. His hair style was very similar to the boxing promoter Don King.

      The David Banner look alike turned into the Incredible Hulk with his conversation. He yelled out, "You wanna be a tough mothafucka. You aint nothing but a hoe. You gonna get to jail and snitch on your homeboy. You are a straight up hoe. Anybody that gotta get up and go hang around another nigga every got damn day just to get him some money is a hoe. Y'all sit around all got damn day and y'all ain't even making no money. You can't buy you no shoes or no clothes. You don't even have enough money to get in the club. Get in the club on the next nigga and gotta sit around and wait on him to buy you drink. Y'all out here doing all these killings and don't have no damn bond money. Stupid muthafucka can't get a paid lawyer. Fighting and killing everyday about nothing. Martin and Malcom just wasted they time. Four and five niggas riding around every day. Four and Five niggas with four or five guns and it's only one shooter. Everywhere y'all go, just out here starting problems. Killing kids cause y'all don't even know how to shoot. Just wasting bullets. That ain't about nothing. Tell me what the fuck is wrong with y'all destroying your own community and killing each other. The KKK don't have to put in work no more. Y'all dumb assess out

The Young and the Reckless

here working for them." He didn't give Demond a chance to respond. He continued a few more seconds and then he walked away like everything was cool.

Demond held on to every word. He thought about how he could use what he had just said and convey a message. He couldn't believe himself. As much as he reached for his phone first to record something he saw. For the first time he just listened with his ears and not his phone. He heard what he said, and he understood where he was coming from even though he was rumbling. He couldn't repeat it word for word, but he got the message loud and clear.

Just then everyone started to arrive. The main two people he was looking for was a no show. He made some phone calls and hadn't received any answers. The guy who was there producing the video asked him did he want to push it back. He noticed he wasn't really into it. He wasn't the energetic person he would see in short video snippets. Just as the producer was waiting on his response someone walked up and asked him why he wasn't with his homeboy, Cinque. He let him know that they had just caught the people who murked his mom and dad. Demond dropped to his knees. He could feel his chest getting tight. When he fell to the ground someone immediately dialed 911.

The paramedics came to the scene. They gave Demond some fluids and told him he was fatigue and had experienced a panic attack. He needed to get some rest. He was exhausted, and his body was letting him know it was time for him to get some rest. The videographer recorded bits and pieces of the ordeal, He had plans to use some of the footage and add it to the to the video once it was done. Demond listened to the details from the producer, rescheduled the video shoot and left to go see about his friend.

The Young and the Reckless

CHAPTER 20

Boom! Crash! Were the sounds Cinque heard at the thunder roared like a lion. Cinque could see lightning flashing through the sky from the window of his bedroom. He had been tossing and turning thinking about the night he went to get in the bed with his parents. All the times before the only images were of the masked men. Tonight, was different. He dreamt of the faces. He starred out of the window and became startled when Neveah entered his room. She crawled in bed with her big brother and rested her head upon his chest.

"Do you ever think about how our lives would be if mom and dad were still here with us?" Neveah waited on her brother to respond.

Cinque raised up from the resting position and propped his hand under his face. He was depicting the well-known photograph of Malcom X. He gave his sister's question some thought.

She continued not without letting him answer the question, "For a long time I missed crawling in the bed with my mom and dad. I know I was young when they died but for whatever reason I didn't go into their room that night. When we first moved here with Uncle Pharaoh, I would go and crawl in bed with him like I did with mom and dad." She chuckled,

"That first night I scared the shit of him. He upped on me too."

"What?" Cinque inquired, "Why didn't you tell me about this before? I didn't know you slept with him. I wanted to go climb in bed with him a many of nights, but I didn't want him to use it against me." Cinque laughed with his hand still propping up his face.

"I just stopped not too long ago. I'll say right before Demond and I started talking. One night I thought to myself Cinque would probably think my uncle was molesting me or something if he caught us on the bed together. Like nights when Paradise would stay, I wouldn't go in there. I think he wanted to tell me to stop because when I woke up a few times he would be on the couch."

Cinque laughed, "I would wonder why he slept on the couch so much."

They both laughed.

"I remember when that dude Kevin mother was killed, and his dad was locked up. Remember Kevin who use to be so fresh when he came to school. I think he lost his mom shortly after we lost mom and dad." Neveah was thinking about one of her classmates.

"Yeah! I remember old dude. I seen him a while back. He gone. I think he started popping those pills and now dude mess with that dog food. He just a young dude too and now he a straight dope fiend." Cinque thought back on how rough Kevin

The Young and the Reckless

must have had it hard after both his parents were not in his reach.

"I'm thankful for Pharaoh. Our uncle may not have it all together, but he has us. I know granny and grandad would have stepped up like most grandparents do. I just wouldn't want to be out there in no man's land." Neveah uttered.

"Some folks get a raw deal. I'm grateful that's not our story. But back to your original question, about mom and dad. I saw Moe and Kevin that night. I get mad because I always think about what I could have done. I could have called the police or anything. I was sleepy, but I went to the bathroom. The next thing I know we were getting in the car with Pharaoh." Cinque took a deep breath, "I hate that they are gone. I often look at grandma and grandpa thinking about our parents. I drift off often thinking about how my life would be. I know I wouldn't be out here being young and reckless. Dad wouldn't have it." He held back the tears continuing to rest his chin on his thumb, "Just so you know, I wouldn't have thought our uncle was doing any thing inappropriate. He not that type of dude. He's just someone that was forced to be parent and he was doing what he knew how to do."

The two of them sat quiet. Neveah pulled the cover up over herself and tucked her self in Cinque's bed. The rain had stopped. The thunder and lightning could no longer be heard or seen. The only sound that could be heard now were the voices from the television coming from Pharaoh's bedroom.

Neveah nodded her head in agreement as she began to dose off. She uttered a few words, "I wonder why mom's side of the family haven't reached out to us."

"They probably have, and Pharaoh was not trying to have it." Cinque didn't give his mom's side of the family another thought. "Neveah, I am going to need you to drop me off down on the set. Demond is having the video shoot tomorrow."

Neveah agreed and was sleep in no time. Cinque wanted to finish discussing about their parents, that night they were killed and the two who were now in jail for the murder of his parents. He figured the storm forced Neveah to come in his room. He was glad she had come in there with him. They hadn't bonded like that in over five years. Neveah often came in the room with him some nights. When she didn't come in his room, he figured she had made it through the night. Pharaoh favored his dad so much it was like he really never left. Xavier and Pharaoh favored in appearance but were night and day. The harsh reality was Xavier was gone. No one could fill his shoes. He would be very disappointed in what Cinque was partaking in with his younger brother. Pharaoh knew Xavier wouldn't approve. Cinque filled the void that Pharaoh felt so empty about. Looking in the face he saw his older brother and it didn't help Cinque possessed the same mannerism of his father. Cinque stared at his sister watching her sleep. He was sleep shortly afterwards.

The Young and the Reckless

Neveah woke up to the smell of breakfast being cooked. She looked at her brother. She thought about what they had discussed. She had so much to say and so much to ask. She wanted to discuss Serenity, but she needed to decide on how she was going to come at him about that situation. She tapped him on the shoulder and told him breakfast was being prepared. She tapped him once more wanting to know what time he needed to be dropped off. He didn't respond. She just concluded she would stay around, so she could take him to the video shoot. She was about to jump fresh just in case she needed to make a guest appearance. Demond hadn't told her any details. She was going to be there because her brother was going to be there. Neveah turned to leave her brother's room.

Cinque walked into the kitchen and noticed Brittany, Pharaoh and Neveah looking like a happy family. They all were sitting down laughing and eating their breakfast. Cinque walked over to the stove to fix his plate. He looked and seen the blueberry Belgium waffles, turkey bacon, scrambled eggs and grits on the stove. He went to grab a plate for the fixings and a small bowl for the grits. He then sat down to join them.

For a brief moment it was though an elephant had entered the room. Everyone was quiet. Then Pharaoh broke the silence. No one was speaking about the arraignment. They all were grieving all over again. A wound that had never quite healed was reopened. No one knew how to feel. The killers were right up under their nose the entire time. In their face and hanging amongst several individuals they considered family.

"I spoke with Coach Porter yesterday. He talked about his plans for the upcoming school year and he wanted to know were you getting ready for college. He's going to bring a list over with some items you will need to get started off the beginning of the school year and Brittany agreed to help me shop." Pharaoh looked to Cinque waiting on his response.

"I'd like for all us to go. Neveah needs to be a part of the experience, so she will know what to expect when it's her turn." Cinque replied.

They conversed about various topics. The only topic that wasn't touched was the arraignment that they were waiting to hear about. The finished their breakfast and Cinque let his sister know he was about to get ready, so she could drop him off.

Neveah pulled up and parked. Demond was standing around with Kavon. He had told everyone the wrong time on purpose. He preferred everyone to be there early than to show up late. Telling them the wrong time had worked out in his favor. Everyone started pulling up around the same time. Several people were in the midst while the setup was taking place. The producer came and told Demond how he was going to arrange things and Demond agreed. While all the commotion was taken place and Demond was performing the lyrics

The Young and the Reckless

while being recorded, Cinque felt his phone vibrating.

"Hello." He waited to hear the voice because the name didn't come across identifying the caller.

"Cinque, are you busy?" Star questioned as she heard the noise in his background.

"I'm at my homeboy video shoot?" Cinque responded to Star as he watched Neveah and Paradise embrace one another. Paradise walked on the block with Rome. The producer had yelled out cut. Demond walked up to Neveah who was standing back watching him. He said a few words to her and kissed her on the lips before he walked away. Cinque tuned back in to the caller that was on his phoneline.

"Okay. I'm at the church and one of my church members is having a hard time with this robot. I know you know who to do this mess. You've won plenty of awards when it comes to dealing with these darn things. You think you can come up to the church at about four to help us out?" Star asked.

"Fa-Show. I'll get one of my homeboys to bring me up there. I'll hit you back when I'm on my way. It's too much noise going on out here and I can barely hear you." Cinque ended the call not hearing if Star had anything else to say.

Cinque was standing near Demond. Demond was telling Cinque he was surprised they had a huge turnout. They looked amongst the crowd and seen Kavon speaking with the producer. Rome walked up as they both were trying to figure out what possible could Kavon be talking about.

"I was just about to come looking for your, Rome." Cinque stated.

"Looking for me what?" Rome was quite confused.

"I just need a ride and I know my homeboys not going to be ready to go and I need to be somewhere today."

"No problem, Que. I got you. You going to love my new ride." Rome smiled like he had just purchased a vehicle off the showroom floor.

Things began to wind down. Cinque followed Rome over to a white Dodge Durango.

"Is it safe to ride in this thing?" Cinque didn't even know why he asked.

"Who you think I am? I learned my lesson. Safety is now my middle name." Rome entered the car and put on his seatbelt. They both laughed.

Cinque began to be Rome's personal GPS. He told him when he would be turning and when he needed to get over to turn. When they pulled up in front of the church Rome just looked around.

"What? You selling work to the pastor?" Rome had a very serious look on his face.

"Dude, no! I'm good so you can go ahead and shake." Cinque said.

The Young and the Reckless

"I'm going to sit right here and make sure you make it safely in. Besides, who's going to dial 911 when the church house catches on fire when you walk through those doors." Rome chuckled.

Cinque put his middle finger up and laughed walking towards the church doors. Rome did as he said. He sat until he couldn't see Cinque any longer.

Cinque found Star in the basement of the church. There had to be some sort of summer camp because there were several children running around. Star introduced Cinque to the young man who was having a rough time with his robot development. Star smiled as she watched Cinque and the young man interact. After a while he started moving about and helping children work on whatever projects they were involved with. When Star noticed Cinque found a resting spot, she went to sit next to him.

"Thank you for coming to help out. I really appreciate it."

"No problem. If you need me, I'm there." Cinque smiled.

"Now that I have you here, I want to talk to you about Serenity." Star waited for his reaction. He didn't blink, and he didn't go into a defense mode. He was ready.

"I have been giving this some thought and I think you need to tell her what your plans are with me. She may not want to hear but you need to be honest. I know that's your child and I can't ignore that you are about to be a father. I know she may even hate me, but you need to be honest with her. You need to be true yourself as well as to her. I know there's a lot going on with you. Waiting to find out how this thing about your parents is about to unfold. I just don't want you to draw a wedge between you and the mother of your future child. As long as you want me around, I'm here."

"Funny that you brought her up. I have been thinking about how I am going to tell her that I'm going to be there for my child. I'm just afraid she's going to be on some type of bull."

"Well, if it gets to that point, the only thing I can suggest if you have to get the courts involved."

"I'm just trying to figure out how am I going to go away to school and be a dad at the same time."

"I just want to know why you didn't use the proper precautions. There is so much birth control available. They have contraceptives all around us. You did know that when you make love, you can make a baby. You did know, that didn't you?" Star was adamant about her question.

"I'm going to talk to her. Can we get out of this church and grab something to eat?"

"Have you gotten a car yet or do you want me to order an Uber?"

"Star, ordered an Uber." Cinque demanded.

The Young and the Reckless

Cinque pulled his cellphone from his pocket. He entered his passcode and scrolled until he reached Serenity's name. Once on her name he chose the option to unblock caller.

CHAPTER 21

Brittany rolled over and grabbed her phone. She had several missed alerts. She was experiencing a persistent feeling of sadness. Her appetite had changed drastically. She had loss total interest in her online publication. She decided to make a YouTube video about what she was undergoing. She rolled over and began to watch Pharaoh as he slept. Tears began to roll down her eyes. She was happy yet sad. In a matter of days, she had formed a relationship with Pharaoh's niece and nephew but had destroyed what little she had with her own son. She couldn't understand why he was ignoring her calls. Before she arrived in St. Louis they talked on a regular basis. She had even attempted to reach out to his dad a few times. She was unsuccessful in contacting him. She figured that he was upset about her relocating without letting him know she was leaving. Now all she could do was wait on the hearing about her a scheduled visitation with her son.

Pharaoh opened his eyes. He stared into Brittany's eyes and noticed her tears. He closed his eyes briefly. He noticed she had been crying excessively. He didn't know what to say. He didn't understand how and why she lost custody of her child. Brittany didn't try to help him understand the situation with her son either.

The Young and the Reckless

"Hey what time is it?" Pharaoh asked.

"It's almost nine." Brittany answered.

"Damn!" Pharaoh hopped up, "I supposed to meet Torrance at the Waffle House at 8:45." He went right in to shower. He was dealing with his on dilemmas. He really couldn't focus on assisting Brittany with hers. He was in and out the shower in less than five minutes. He exited from the bathroom shower entering his bedroom soak and wet.

"Brittany, I forgot to ask you did you have something to do today?" before she could respond with her agenda, he told her what he needed her to do, "My cleaning man is coming over to sweep the house. I need you to watch his every move while he runs through the house. Then call me when he's done. He is supposed to be here around 9:30. I should be done or just about done. So, I just don't know how long this thing with Torrance is going to take. I may go pick up Que a car. I know he's tired of bumming rides from everybody." He dried himself as he gave Brittany the simple instructions.

Brittany agreed, and Pharaoh was on his way out the door to meet Torrance. He wanted to get to his destination before Torrance arrived. In all his years he had never arrived at the designated time, he was always there fifteen to thirty minutes before. He pulled on the parking lot of the Waffle House in Berkeley. It was exactly 8:45 and Torrance was already there. He could see him sitting near the window drinking coffee as he parked his car. Pharaoh placed his hands in the praising position on the steering wheel of his vehicle. He didn't know what to expect and being that the killers of his brother and sister-in-law had been up under his nose the entire time had him feeling some type of way. To make matters worse his brother was killed with the first gun Pharaoh had ever purchased. As a child he was fascinated with lions. He had lions on everything. Menace II Society was his favorite movie but so was Lion King. He just didn't watch it as much. He kind of forgot about his fascination with lions until he thought about his first gun.

Pharaoh wondered about what his brother had to be thinking once he saw that gun. The last time he spoke with his brother he was thinking about running for the Alderman in his community. He was on a mission to clean up the community that he had contributed to destroying. While Xavier was off into the church life, he was rubbing elbows with a lot of connected officials. He was on a road to redemption.

Xavier discussed his new plans with Torrance first one Sunday he had left church. It was not intentional that Torrance had heard about his plans first it was just that he had bumped into him first. Torrance let him know that he was behind him one hundred percent. Pharaoh didn't seem to agree with his brother's future plans. When Xavier mentioned Torrance was down, Pharaoh wanted to know why Torrance heard about this plan first. He didn't know how long cleaning up and the community was going to take, and he didn't care about the details. He wanted to make sure the money kept coming in and that's what all had mattered to him.

The Young and the Reckless

Xavier began telling everyone how he was about to change things around. He wanted to leave some impressionable footprints in the world. Pharaoh thought about when he asked him was, he planned on becoming President of the United States. When Xavier looked him in his eyes with the sincerest look and replied, "I just might or try to get close to it." Pharaoh knew he meant what he was saying. Now he sat in the car wondering if that was why his brother lost his life because cats didn't know how they were going to eat if Xavier took the legal route. Xavier was proposing a propaganda for peace and Pharaoh was still wanting to flood the streets with the poison.

Torrance exited from the restaurant. He let his waitress know he was about to step outside for a few minutes. He approached Pharaoh's car. He observed him with his eyes closed and his hands placed together, resting on the steering wheel. He watched him for a few minutes. Through the tinted windows he noticed a few tears strolling down both of his cheeks. He slowly tapped on Pharaoh's car window. Pharaoh slightly jumped when he heard the first tap. He became startled from his thoughts as Torrance tapped on the driver side window. Pharaoh turned the car off and opened the car door. He stood from the car and looked at Torrance, "I'm having a little moment."

"I know dude. That's why I said let's go grab some breakfast, so we can sit down and talk. I know you like preparing breakfast for everyone for fun. What's better than having breakfast in one of the spots we use to hangout frequently." Torrance was speaking about when they first started hustling and after being on the block all night, they would run to the very same Waffle House. Everything was the same when they first started hanging out there. The only changes were the workers.

Pharaoh followed Torrance back into the restaurant. As they sat down the waitress came over to the table and asked them were, they ready to place their order. Torrance placed his order first, "I will have the pecan waffle with the hash brown bowl with American chess and hold the pork." He looked up at Pharaoh. He was still holding the menu. He knew whatever was on his mind that kept him in the car was still bothering him. "My mans will have the same thing." Torrance gave his menu to the waitress and so did Pharaoh.

"Dude, what's troubling you? I know you were going through since you got that news. But I promise you I'm going to handle this. Those boys will get touched. This is already handle. I'm on it."

"Remember when we were kids and we were playing near that lake and when we ran across it. That water was too deep for me. I wasn't tall enough. I was damn near drowning. Xavier turned around and seen I wasn't behind him. When he seen me struggling, he ran back to get me. I can remember you standing in the mist looking so afraid. Xavier had this look in his eyes. His chin was trembling, and eyes were dim. He has always had this look of shine in eyes. Que has that same look to me, but that day it was different. I can't say it was a look a fear. His eyes told me he had me. We never spoke about that day. He didn't even tell my mother. He had handled

The Young and the Reckless

it. All I can think about what he was thinking when he saw my strap. I know he saw. Knowing those niggas, they probably made sure he saw it too."

Torrance didn't know what to say. He knew his friend was going through it, but he didn't know to what extent. Listening to him talk was giving him a clear understanding. He didn't know how much of it he could handle but he continued to listen.

Pharaoh continued, "I just want to talk to Moe and Kevin. I have several questions but the biggest one of all is why. I helped them niggas eat. It's a doggy dog world I tell you. I know he wouldn't be happy with me about Que, but I've done right by him with Neveah. I have my reasons for Que but it's some selfish shit. With Que it's like Xavier never left. I'm glad that Coach in his life though. He is showing him some shit that Xavier would be showing him if he were here. Since that news dropped, I straight been stand offish with Brittany. She is going through that shit with her son. She doesn't even mention him by name. I can tell it's bothering her."

Torrance was waiting on him to stop talking. He was sitting like a little girl trying to enter the jump rope has her friends turned. He was trying to come into the conversation.

The waitress came back to their table with their food. Pharaoh thanked her and asked for some orange juice. She asked them did everything look good and they agreed that it did. Before she walked away Pharaoh asked for some warm syrup. She let him know she would be right back with the orange juice and syrup. Torrance watched as she walked away. He looked around the restaurant scanning the faces of every individual in the place. He had sat in the back, so he could watch the door. He was strapped, and he wondered had Pharaoh totted his gat. Most likely his wasn't but he wasn't sure. He knew if he didn't have it on him, he had it in his car. He was only concerned because it was an individual that had been watching them. He didn't look familiar, but it was odd to him the way he kept staring. He didn't want to mention it to Pharaoh because he didn't want him to turn and look back. He gave the guy one more look over and said to himself he was going to keep his eye on him. He brought his attention back to Pharaoh. His longtime friend had appeared to be a little distant lately.

The young lady returned with the items requested and the two gentlemen began to eat their food. Torrance decided to get his words in since Pharaoh had taken a break from talking.

"I like Coach Porter. He's a good dude. He seems genuine. I don't remember having teachers like that in school. Stuff different these days. These teachers have to wear a lot of hats nowadays and they don't even get paid their worth." Pharaoh chewed and shook his head in agreement as Torrance talked.

"Moe and Kevin surprised me. Really Kevin though. Moe has always been a grimy dude, but Kevin I just can't believe it. Well not so much believe but Moe must have hung dangled something over him. I just don't know what. I have been thinking about how did they get that gun. I been trying to

The Young and the Reckless

figure that out for the longest." Torrance chewed in between his words.

Pharaoh looked up, "That's what troubling me. I don't even know how long the gun been missing. I'm mad at myself. How I let that slip up. I thought about the few times we had them at the spot. I only keep coming back that Kevin and you are the only ones that really were down there in that basement with the gun collection when I had mugs around."

Torrance instantly became offended. He became very defensive. He didn't know what to say at this point. He knew he had to say something. He knew Pharaoh was hurt but to think he would betray him was beyond him.

"I know you are hurt and upset. I know that finding out who is behind it all is rehashing old feelings. As far as me, I loved Xavier as though he was my brother. I know I don't have to tell you how I feel about you."

The moment he said how I feel about you the waitress approached the table. She had a bewildered look in her eyes, "Y'all okay. Do you guys need anything else?"

Pharaoh continued to eat, and Torrance let her know that they were good. He watched her as she walked away. She went over to another one of her coworkers. She whispered to the other female and she immediately looked over in Pharaoh and Torrance's direction.

Torrance chuckled, "That broad probably thinks we are couple."

Pharaoh turned to look back at the two women. While taking a look at the females, he noticed the same individual that Torrance had been making eye contact with since he had entered the restaurant.

"You see dude sitting back there. I know his face from somewhere." Pharaoh mumbled with food in his mouth.

The individual gathered himself and walked over to the table. Torrance placed his hand on his weapon as the gentleman approached the table.

"I was sitting over there trying to think where I knew you two from. Then it hit me. Xavier people. If I was in my suit and tie you all could have placed me. I seen you checking me out." The gentlemen spoke directly to Torrance. He was a tall with a caramel complexion. His teeth were perfect. He smelled like money. The gentleman continued to speak, "I'm Xavier's homeboy from the church. Xavier and I had major plans for this city. We lost a good man when he died, He carried a great deal of information when he left. I wish I had more time to pick his brain."

Pharaoh reached out to give him a handshake. Torrance dapped him up too. Then Pharaoh asked him did have a card. The gentlemen gave him a card and Pharaoh said, "I'll be in touch. I might be interested in finishing what my brother was trying to start."

The Young and the Reckless

The gentleman let Pharaoh know he looked forward to hearing from him. Pharaoh looked at the business card and read the name Ruble Steele. He slightly jogged away. He was dressed for a jog. Torrance watched him as he took his seat back at his table.

"I know that dude and it just ain't from no church. We didn't hangout at no church with Xavier. I know his face from somewhere." Torrance said as he reached for the card, "I'm gonna put my people on this Ruble Steele." He handed Pharaoh back the card. "I called you out here to see how you were doing ang to let you know what I found out about Brittany. I knew she would probably be at the house and I didn't want her eavesdropping thinking you investigating her."

Pharaoh was wide open, "What's the word?"

"You know I be fucking with that lil police broad, Shelly? She was telling me that the department got word she was back in town dealing with a custody battle. They want to investigate her about that check cashing place that burned down during those Ferguson riots. They believe her, and friends got some major bread behind that and then they burned the building down. Surveillance cameras in the area allegedly has them fleeing the scene right before the building began to burn. They have been trying to get all the recordings from cameras in the vicinity of the check cashing place."

"I never asked her about that, but it makes sense. They probably got that bread. Can't blame 'em though. We probably would have done the same. I know that online magazine ain't doing numbers like that. You have to have a product. Like where's the residual income. She cool though. It's just the situation with her son. She good with Nevaeh. Que loves her. Speaking of Que. I have to get dude a new car before he leaves for Indiana. He out here bumming rides. Dude so humble he hasn't even mentioned anything about a car." Pharaoh looked at his phone. He noticed it was a little after 9:30.

"You plan on going to the arraignment hearing?" Torrance asked already knowing the answer.

Pharaoh sent a text message trying to see if the dude had arrived to clean the place. He looked up from his phone, "I'm not sure if I really want to go. I haven't even talked to my mom and dad about it. She's dealing with my dad right now. It's cancer. He has his good days where he's up and moving around and then there are the days where he just lays around all day."

"Damn dude. I didn't know you had all that going on. I see the weight of the world is on your shoulders right now." Torrance muttered.

Brittany stood in the living room looking as the guy parked. She text Pharaoh, *he just pulled up*, as she went to open the door. When she looked up, she was taken by surprise. The one individual she

The Young and the Reckless

was trying to get in contact with but couldn't locate him.

"Hey, Jarvis." She said.

Jarvis looked up in total shock. He almost dropped his black bag full of equipment. He was trying to figure out why the mother of his child was currently at one of his client's home. "Hey, Brittany." He response was dry.

"I was expecting to see you while I was at court trying to fight for custody of our son." Brittany figured she said just enough to engage him in the conversation of why he wasn't there in court himself.

"Well, my mom pretty much gotten me out the way. It's *No Limit* to what she will do to keep our son away from me. She cares more about him than she does me and she gave birth to me." Jarvis shook his head.

"I guess she's trying to correct her wrongs and ensure he doesn't take the path you did. I get it. I just don't understand why she doesn't want me to be a part of his life. She had him all the time and I just visited him. We agreed on that and then she crosses me. She sat in court and didn't look in my direction. My son didn't even look at me when he was on the stand. I couldn't understand what happened." Brittany was holding back her tears.

"My mom is like the oppressor. She's very similar to someone who wants you to remain unhealthy, ignorant and addicted to some sort of drug. She has her foot on my neck and it's light enough for me to make a few moves." Jarvis attempted to grab security equipment from the black bag he was carrying. He appeared to be slightly agitated speaking about his mother as he thought about how conniving should could be. He continued to talk, "I didn't go to court because my mother and I have an agreement. I cannot believe my dad doesn't say anything about her crazy way. I take that back. Yes, I can. She controls my dad, so I'm pretty much left to defend myself in the matter."

Brittany didn't know what to say. She knew he probably wanted to know why she had run off, but she didn't want to discuss it. She began to wonder what type of relationship in which Jarvis and Pharaoh had. Her thoughts were all over the place.

Jarvis moved about the house during his normal routine. Brittany began to notice how he moved freely about the house. He appeared to know the house better than she did. She noticed Jarvis had maintained his workout regimen. Even in a black polo style shirt and khakis you could see his toned muscles.

When he reached the bedroom, Brittany decided to let him do that part alone. She had watched him enough. Then she thought about Pharaoh asking her had she followed him like he instructed. She also wanted to know what all Pharaoh was in to being that he had someone scanning home.

"When did you start doing this type of work?" Brittany asked as she waved hand circling around to some up what he was doing standing in the doorway just enough where she could watch him.

The Young and the Reckless

"When I was locked up people were talking about all types of ways to remain employed and I knew a few dudes who got jammed up on wiretaps, so I took some business courses. Then I invested in my merchandise. I also do pest control. I make majority of my money in North and South county. People are concerned with the rodents that comes from those fields in certain areas. I like the outdoors, so I just created my own lane." Jarvis was proud of his accomplishments.

"That's pretty cool." Was all Brittany could muster up.

"How long have you been back? Jarvis asked.

Brittany was trying to remember if he had just asked that question. Then she heard the garage door open. Neveah was talking very loudly. She couldn't make out what she was saying but she heard her talking. Jarvis had finished up in the bedroom and was heading towards the basement.

"Hey, Jarvis." Neveah spoke and so did Paradise.

Brittany was appalled. She wanted to know just how much Jarvis knew about the family she had taken up residence.

"Hey Neveah and Paradise. How have you all been since the accident?" Jarvis asked.

Paradise responded, "I'm blessed and thankful to have a ride or die friend. She never left me side."

"That's good. It's nice seeing you two. Let me go ahead and finish my work. I'm running behind schedule. Jarvis finished the work and before he left, he handed Brittany one of his business cards.

Brittany had several more questions for Jarvis. She felt that they had a lot of unanswered questions. Jarvis had plenty, but he respected Pharaoh. He was the first one that accepted his business proposal and he had put him in contact with a whole team of people that generated him a lucrative income. He knew once he gave Brittany that card, she would contact him. He was going to let Pharaoh know himself about the connection he and Brittany had.

Brittany texted Pharaoh to let him know the guy was done and they needed to talk.

Pharaoh looked at his phone. He looked up at Torrance. "This breakfast was great. You want to follow me, so I can go pick out Que a car? I want to surprise him with a new whip."

"I can just ride with you and come back to pick up my ride when we are done." Torrance retorted.

"I'll just follow you to drop your car off, so you want have to come way back out here to pick it up. Then we can go to this car lot. I already know what I want to get him."

CHAPTER 22

Pharaoh paced back and forth. He pondered on the night he lost his brother and sister-in-law. He became weak and weary. Pharaoh's first feeling was the image of his brother being in fear for his family became frightening. He was trying to take all this in and figure out how did Moe get a hold of his gun. He thought about what his brother might have thought when he seen the army green gun with the lion imaged embedded in the handle. He began to think that maybe Torrance wasn't so loyal. How was he going to come at him and let him know he backdoored him. He contemplated with how he would come at him or what would he say. If he really backdoored him this wouldn't be a talking type of situation. This situation needed to be bodied and fast. He was preparing for court when he got the call. He began to have all kinds of thoughts. He wanted to some one to blame and right now blaming Torrance felt good. He quickly let the thought of Torrance backdooring him go. He knew Torrance was loyal. Xavier had looked out for Torrance the same way he had looked out for him.

Pharaoh had found out the time and day Moe and Kevin were being arraigned. They were about to have a formal reading of the crime they were being charged with. He decided they wouldn't attend that arraignment. They all needed to be mentally prepared for that.

Pharaoh had attempt to self-medicate his depression. He had some serous issues that needed to be unpacked with a professional After losing his brother he did attempt to change his behavior. He let as though there was nothing left to los. He knew he had two individuals to look after and he couldn't do that properly.

He was slightly pleased when he heard Moe and Kevin had both entered a guilty plea. Moe Jackson, of St. Louis, pleaded guilty of murder and other crimes in the shooting of Xavier and Bria Tyson. He was originally charged with two counts of first-degree murder.

Kevin Terrell pleaded guilty to two counts of second-degree murder along with five counts of armed criminal action, two counts of assaulting a law enforcement officer. Kevin had fired several shots towards the police officers when they responded to the forty-two hundred block of Red Bud Ave. He grazed one police officer. A bullet ricocheted and grazed one of the officers as he tried to run down the alley to get way. They were both had to wait on their trial date. The prosecuting attorney was pushing for a life sentence with no eligibility for parole. Keven was trying to get a lighter plea deal. Keven informed his public defender that the entire ordeal was planned by Moe. The Prosecuting District Attorney was not budging. She was going to see to it that they both were getting a sentence of life without.

The Young and the Reckless

Pharaoh was okay with himself for not attending the arraignment. He wasn't ready to relive the worse day of his life again. He spoke with his parents and they were pleased. He was happy to hear that his daddy was doing much better. He was making plans to spend more time with him. What was on his mind was Torrance.

They had to be thinking of each other because he watched Torrance as he approached the door. He reached to open the door. He opened the door and walked away to sit down. He said to himself remain calm and keep your composure. He knew Moe had been in and out of jail. He didn't quite understand what he was being charged with doing his short bids. He would do two or three years and be back home. His crimes were more so that he violated his probation.

"I have been thinking about how they got a hold to your gun. Dude I fucked up. Kevin asked me about some guns when we were at the spot one day and I just told him to grab one. I didn't check to see what he grabbed, nor did I ask him what he needed it for. I know he or Moe could have gotten a strap from anywhere. Man, I'm fucked up behind this and I feel partly responsible." Torrance was being completely honest, and Pharaoh knew it. He felt bad for even thinking his friend was responsible. He let those feelings go. He walked over to embrace his childhood friend. They both stood there crying. Pharaoh left the Waffle House knowing that Torrance wasn't behind the death of his family He didn't know how to feel but he knew Torrance had to be beating himself up for being so careless. He wondered how long he had pondered on the incident to make him remember.

Brittany entered the room they occupied. She walked up and joined in, "I understand you all might be having a male bonding moment, but yawl really need to see about Cinque and Neveah."

Pharaoh stepped back and looked Brittany directly in her eyes, "I don't even know what to say to them. I don't know what they expected from all this."

Brittany looked Pharaoh over, "Baby, I truly understand. Neither one of us kind find the words. But, the first thing that I will suggest is that you all need to see a therapist. You all need someone to assist in the healing process. It's not saying you all are crazy or anything. If you hurt your hand you go to the doctor, if your head hurts you may take a pain pill but what do you do when your heart and soul are hurt?"

Pharaoh understood exactly what Brittany was telling him. Torrance even gave what she said some thought.

"Dude, she's right. This can't continue to go ignored. We can find it easy to gravitate towards out of sight out of mind. We typically ignore mental illness and that must be changed. I'll set up the appointments and let you know what you need to do afterwards."

Pharaoh agreed and walked his friend to the door. He was disappointed in himself to think his friend would cross him. He was upset all over again.

The Young and the Reckless

He needed someone else to blame. For a long time, he thought about what he would do if he ever found out who committed the murder. It didn't go as planned for him, but he was thankful that they were caught. He knew it was time to making some changes. He was going to start with his main source of income. Before Torrance left, he let him know that he needed to have a conversation with Kevin.

CHAPTER 23

Cinque stood in front of Serenity's front door. She knew he had been standing there. Her neighbor Ms. Tina called and let her know he had pulled up in his uncle's car. Serenity sent her little brother to open the door. She didn't want Cinque to change his mind about seeing her being that he hadn't even bring himself to knock on the door. Cinque asked her little brother where she was, but her brother didn't reply. He walked away as though he had a problem with Cinque. He did. Serenity walked to the door as though she was surprise to see him standing there.

"I guess you wanna talk to me know?" She asked with a noticeable attitude.

Cinque looked her up and down. She was very much pregnant. He didn't know how far a long she was, so he asked, "How many months are you?"

"I'm twenty-seven weeks." She said as she placed her hand on her belly.

Cinque tried to calculate the weeks knowing that four weeks equals one month. He became aggravated and thought to himself that stopping by to see her wasn't a good idea.

"Do you need anything?" he asked.

She wanted to tell him she wasn't worried about her needing anything when his uncle forced

The Young and the Reckless

her to leave their home. She decided to choose her words carefully, "Que, I must apologize. When I barged in your home, I was under the assumption that you had those guys break in my home. Why I thought that I don't know. On that day those guys were all over the news and my dad had been arrested. He has two do six months. His parole officer violated his parole due to him being around his cousin who was a convicted felon. I wasn't thinking that day. Being pregnant is messing with my emotions. My mom still doing the same things. I just have a lot to deal with."

Cinque didn't know rather to tell her the real reason he had stopped by. He had listened to her plead her case and figured she had enough to deal with. Then he thought about Star. He wanted to report back to her how he had the talk with Serenity. He knew he couldn't leave without accomplishing what he originally came there for in the first place.

Cinque looked around and noticed the gentle breeze. He felt a calmness. He took a deep breath and began to speak, "Serenity, you may not like what I'm about to say to you, but I have to be honest." He looked at her and she raised one eyebrow becoming attuned with him holding on to every word. He continued, "We should have taken better precautions when we were being intimate. Neither one of us is a prepared to become someone's parent. You are not financially prepared, and my line of work isn't promising. How can we properly care for a child when we can't properly care for ourselves? I know it's too late to talk about what we should have done when this child is on the way.

I just want you to know that I am going to support my child in any way I can. I'm expecting us to be able to co-parent this child. I hope we can remain friends through the process."

Serenity looked at him and she understood what he was saying. She had been mad at him for avoiding her calls and cutting her off as though they never had what they once had. She looked him dead in his eyes, She was hurt by what he said but she knew he meant it. Holding back her tears she responded, "I understand. Friends we are and friends we will be." She closed her front door and walked away. It wasn't what she wanted it to be. She realized his heart was somewhere else. She seen it in his eyes that day he left her sitting in the car to go speak to the girl she saw at the church. That look was the reason she deleted the number from his cellphone.

CHAPTER 24

Brittany stood looking in the refrigerator. She was trying to wait on Pharaoh to get off the phone with Torrance. As soon as she was about to speak, he would call right back. She didn't know what they had going on, but it was beginning to irritate her. She was upset about what was going on with her child and to make matters worse Pharaoh hadn't even seemed to acknowledge it was a problem. She figured it would be best if she would just leave. Then she thought about it her decision and realized she was being irrational. She hadn't contacted any of her friends to let them know she was in St. Louis. She hadn't even reached out to her little brother to see how he was holding up. She had fallen off and she had been down long enough. She appreciated Pharaoh being there for her while she was going through her dilemma while he was dealing with his own dilemma. She closed the refrigerator door and turned around to face Pharaoh.

"I have been meaning to tell you about your cleaning guy." She stated. She now had his undivided attention.

"What about him? Was there an issue when he came by?" Pharaoh inquired.

"I don't know if we can consider him being the father of my child an issue. I just wanted you to know that. I was quite surprised when I opened the door and saw that it was him."

"That's crazy>" Pharaoh was shocked that he didn't even pay attention to that. When he heard she had a child he didn't bother finding out by who. He continued, "One day he came by and he was telling me about how his mom was so controlling. You know she makes him call ahead to see if he can hang out with his own son? Man, so Jarvis is your BD. He is a cool dude. I like him, and I don't say that about everybody. What did he say when he saw you?"

"He didn't ask me anything. We talked about the court situation briefly while he worked and once, he was done he just left."

"I can respect that. Does he know that you and I are together?"

Brittany looked at him and smiled. She didn't know what they were calling what they had going on and, on the day, she told him her child's father was in his home he let her know they were together. "So, this here is official?" she pointed her finger back and forth between the two of them.

He walked over closer to her and took her into his arms. He looked down into her and eyes and she looked up into his eyes. He began to speak, "From now own I'm going to do a better job at making you understand where you stand in my life."

"That's fine and I appreciate that." She smiled and continued to speak, "What you need to do is go down stairs and let Kavon line you up. You

The Young and the Reckless

beginning to look a little rough around the edges." Brittany laughed as she kissed him on his lips.

Kavon shut the clippers off. He then turned the styling chair around and handed Cinque the mirror. Cinque looked at his hair. He admired his lil Boosie fade and the fresh lining.

"That dude know he cold with those clippers." Demond watched as Cinque checked himself out. Demond stood up to admire his cut that Kavon and just completed before he let Cinque sit in the chair.

"We never got a chance to talk about that night you dipped out the club with Star. What happened to those dudes that hopped down on you?" Kavon asked Cinque.

"Man, that was wild night. I was just trying to make sure Star was straight. I just knew she was going to stop messing with me behind that crazy incident. She was scared as hell. I had her running down streets, hitting gangways and running through alleys. We got away though." Cinque recalled the events of the night of his graduation. Besides being shot at the biggest thing he remembered was only trying to remain calm so Star wouldn't panic and get them caught up.

"Did you find out who it was that got up on you?" Demond asked already knowing the answer to his question. He just wanted to know if Cinque had seen who it was. He was looking for some sort of confirmation.

Cinque didn't want to spend much time talking about that dreadful night. He was grateful things turned out the way it did for him. He thought about when old boy came back for Caine in *Menace II Society.* Caine wasn't so lucky. He was gunned down on the day he was supposed to be moving to another city in search of new beginnings. Although it was a movie, that's likely how things happened. Karma comes back full circle. This time around Cinque's story ended differently. He and his girl ware okay. They were both shook up from being shot at but the lived to see another day.

In a few days he would be leaving for Indiana. He was headed to college and he was going to get to do what he enjoyed and that was play ball. He was about to leave behind all the rigamarole he had been caught up with for the last few years of his life. That night was behind him. He made it home safely and that was all that mattered to him.

Demond continued, "Somebody saw you in traffic and said the next thing they know someone was trying to get at you. I didn't get the call until after I was done performing. My phone died while I was on stage. When I got to the car, I charged my phone. I had all kinds of missed calls. I was trying to figure out why Pharaoh and Torrance had dipped out so fast. Then I figured it out what had gone once my phone came back on. Neveah let me know you were okay."

Cinque drifted off in his thoughts. He could hear Demond, but he wasn't really wasn't giving thought to the conversation. He began to think about Star. Cinque and let her know that he had the

The Young and the Reckless

conversation with Serenity. He let her know it went better than he expected. She was pleased, and it now made sense to why Serenity had sent her a friend request.

"Que!" Pharaoh yelled from the top of the steps.

"What's up, Unk?" Cinque responded.

"Let me holla at you for a second."

Cinque headed up the stairs with Kavon and Demond in tow.

Cinque made it to the top of the stairs. Brittany, Neveah and Pharaoh stood in the kitchen looking very questionable. He didn't know what was going on. He was afraid to ask. They were looking very weird and he didn't know why. Then they all laughed.

Pharaoh walked to the front door, "Follow me outside young man."

Everyone followed Pharaoh out of the door. While they all poured out of the standing in the front yard, Torrance pulled up in a white Chevrolet Equinox.

Cinque knew it was for him. He walked right up to the truck, "I thought you were going have me something new the day I graduated but this was worth the wait. I see you don't want me out her flossing in your Benz anymore."

Torrance opened the truck door, "Get in."

Cinque entered his new vehicle and looked around. He laughed when he saw the car seat in the back seat.

He had lost the faith when he lost his parents, but Star had helped him to restore it. He was about to put his young and reckless ways to behind him and face his new challenges head on.

Pharaoh walked up to the truck and closed the door. He smiled at his nephew, "We are going to have to get you some tint before you leave for Indiana. Real niggas don't ride fishbowl."

Acknowledgments

First and foremost, I want to thank God for blessing me with this gift. I know without Him none of you would be holding this book in your hand. Next up is YOU! Yes, you, I would like to thank you for letting me take up a few hours of your time. Because of people like you, I know that my gift is appreciated. So, I simply want to express my gratitude and appreciation., I thank you for the support.

Please feel free and email me with your thoughts at booksbyteresaseals@gmail.com

Teresa Seals

Coming Soon

All for Love

Teresa Seals

Chapter 1

August 2017

    Melody shoved her Macy's department store bags behind the passenger seat of her black SUV, making sure it was hidden out of sight. Being addicted to online retail was her current drug of choice. She'd often have her packages sent to the retailer than her place of residence. Melody found it easier to hide her bags from the mall rather than the packages that arrived directly at her front door.

    She swiftly entered the vehicle not partaking in her usual routine. She usually would get in her vehicle, and before she pulled off, she'd place the track on number three of Yo Gottti's *I Am* cd. The day was different. Melody had one thing on her mind and it wasn't Yo Gotti. Today, Melody had to hit the road in a matter of hours and being that she had made several promises to her grandmother she needed to come through on

All for Love

before she was on the road. Her grandmother was the last person on this side of creation she would let down.

In less than twenty minutes, Melody had maneuvered through traffic from South County to the city of North St. Louis. She had her grandmother's meal from Panda Express as she exited her vehicle expeditiously entering her childhood home. She found her grandmother sitting in her blue rocking chair in front of the television watching one of her soaps. They spoke briefly and she let her grandmother know she would call her when she had reached Springfield. She was back out the door headed home to pack for her brief business trip.

Melody trotted off the porch and hopped back in her SUV. She revved the engine and was back on her mission. She slammed on her breaks immediately and threw the truck in park in the middle of the street. She noticed a piece of trash on her windshield that wasn't there before. The trash was a small torn piece of crumpled up brown paper bag that read.

Call me at 342-3434. We need to talk.

Melody looked around to see if anyone she knew was around outside. She saw no one and figured the note could not have been for her. If they really wanted her, they would have knocked on the door. She was puzzled for a moment trying to figure out why whoever left the note couldn't wait for to come back outside. She wasn't in her grandmother's house no longer than five minutes. She put the note in her pocket, got back in her vehicle and headed home.

The way Melody had driven her vehicle within the last hour, she was thankful that STL's finest was nowhere in the vicinity she had been traveling. She made it safely in her driveway parked with a few minutes to spare to pack for her trip. She left her Macy's bag hidden and made her way in the house. She noticed the door had been left open, so she didn't have to locate her key or knock to be let in her home. Melody never could find her door key majority of the time. It's a good thing someone was always there, or she would find herself locked out of her own home.

"I don't know why, every time I have an out of town speaking engagement, I wait until the last minute to pack. I must do better with myself." The statement rolled of Melody tongue loudly with frustration as she walked down the hallway to her bedroom.

"I never thought it was last minute. I just assume that this is one of your crazy methods of doing things. I have always been under the assumption that you think about all your mess, do a process of elimination and throw all the items

All for Love

that make the cut in your suitcase." Bennie said as he stared at the screen of his cellphone.

"I do think about what I want to take." Melody spoke in a matter of fact tone, "The only problem I have is putting my hands right on it." Melody stood staring into her closet.

"What time do you have to be in Springfield?" Bennie asked with his eyes glued to his cellphone.

"We can't check-in to our hotel room until three. It's a four-hour drive. So, I say we can leave with-in the next hour and make there by five." Melody said placing a few items in her suitcase.

"I'm about to smoke before we hit the highway. Just let me know when you ready and I will put your luggage in the car." Bennie exited the room. He was headed to the garage. One of Melody's house rule is no smoking in the house. She was about to ask him had he packed but she remembered she noticed his suitcase when she first walked in the house.

"I do think about what I want to take. The only problem I have is putting my hands right on it." Melody stood staring into her closet, thinking about what items to remove and grab quickly knowing she didn't really need them anyway. Her items were already in the vehicle. Melody already had to figure out how to pack the packages she had hidden in her vehicle. She had just bought four outfits. One outfit for business and three casual yet business depending on the type of shoe she chooses. At times she considered herself to be fashionista but she's more comfortable in sweats, t-shirts and flip-flops.

Melody was headed to the door but seen Bennie coming back towards the bedroom. She stopped in the hallway closet pretending to search for an unknown item.

"What time do we have to be in Springfield?" Bennie asked with his eyes still glued to his cellphone.

"We can't check-into our hotel room until three. It's a four-hour drive. So, I will say we can leave with-in the next thirty-minutes and make it there by five." Melody said as she grabbed some toiletries to place in her suitcase.

Bennie headed the opposite way back down the hall toward the garage and Melody waited to hear the garage door close before she ran to retrieve her recent purchases. She was only keeping her purchases a secret from her fiancé because her awaiting reward for her weight loss journey would be a new wardrobe at his expense.

Four hours later Melody and Bennie had made it to the parking lot of the upscale luxury

All for Love

University Plaza Hotel and Convention Center. The hotel was the central located near Missouri State University. Melody agreed to checking into the hotel as Bennie went to meet up with two of his neighborhood friends who had relocated to Springfield after being released from a medium security correctional facility.

Melody made her way through the revolving glass door of the hotel, with her purse in tow, headed straight to the front desk. She spoke with the receptionist, pulled out her identification and her form of payment. She was handed the keys to her suite where she and Bennie would be for the next three days. This was a business trip during the day and a mini vacation during the night for them.   Melody decided to locate the room to the workshops she would be attending and the one event room where she would give her presentation.

The three days passed by quickly. Melody presentation was remarkable. She was asked to comeback with more days to present at the Educational Leadership conference. She and Bennie were back on the road. She looked through her photos on her phone. She decided to place her favorite photo of her and Bennie on her social media platform. It was the picture of the two of them having dinner that Bennie friend Andre had taken of them smiling very intimately. Melody uploaded the picture with the caption, *we go back like bombers boo in the coldest weather.* Those were the lyrics to Ja Rule and Ashanti's *Always On Time.*

    Melody dropped her phone in the cup holder after posting the picture, let her seat back and was about to fall asleep. Bennie called her name and asked her to hook her phone up to the car, so her playlist could play as he drove for the four hours. She agreed and immediately fell asleep. When she opened her eyes, they were pulling in their drive way. She asked Bennie to go get her some Baskin Robbins. He agreed and let her know he had to make a stop first and he'd grabbed her favorite pint of freshly packed jamoca almond fudge.

    Melody looked at him before he pulled off. He already knew what the look was for, so he made his way out of the SUV and opened the door. They shared a laugh before he was about to make his run. Melody sat her purse and phone down on the kitchen table, headed down the hallway right to the bathroom. When she was done taking care of her business, she went to retrieve her cell phone. As she grabbed her phone, the phone was timing out, but she noticed she had a message from messenger. She didn't recognize the name, so she placed her thumb on the button, but it didn't recognize her thumbprint. Just in a matter of seconds Melody grew angry with frustration

All for Love

and immediately hit the button and now she just entered her six-digit code. She immediately clicked on her messenger icon. Melody didn't even notice the name. The message had taken her back.

I really ain't Tryna create any drama in your life or mine but we have been put in a situation where Bennie is a common denominator and I don't believe u are aware but we have a child sue in less than 2 weeks and I've been Tryna cordial but now it's the end and he need to man up

She sat down on her gray sofa. Melody read the message twelve more times before she responded with her message of…. *Why are you contacting me exactly?*

She didn't know what to think. Her first thought that the individual maybe had message the wrong individual. She assumed that there was no way in the world that Bennie could have cheated with an individual who couldn't properly form a sentence. Then she thought about the phone number from the paper that was left on her windshield. As she was headed to retrieve the phone number her phone buzzed letting her know she received another message.

Because u are his excuse for Neva being available to do things that need to be done to prepare for the arrival of this child so now that u know things should run a bit more smoothly I assume

Teresa Seals

Melody was in disbelief. She was ready to call the grammar police. At this point she was ready to fight Bennie on the caliber of trash he had possibly conceived a child with. Melody responded with....

They will never run smoothly, and you can contact me after DNA has been completed.

For a second Melody thought the individual was just simply doing her own version of shorthand. After she received the next message she thought to herself, "this bitch got to be retarded."

Look if y'all want drama I will most definitely give it to y'all and DNA is a must so do u want me to put the red bud address on the papers or yours cause I was prepared for that and I'm ready for drama so it would be in yall best interest to make everything cordial but suit yoself shit it's ball time now
cause u hip as mfka but I'm done wit the text now everybody on the same page the ball in my court

Melody stared at the message and her high yellow complexion became a bright pinkish red. Her eyes were a burning fury that couldn't form a tear. She sent her last message and threw her phone.

Bitch I didn't fuck you. Drama? My best interest? You got me fucked! ✌

All for Love

    Melody screenshotted the first message she received from the Remy Martin individual and sent it directly to Bennie with the caption…. EXPLAIN.

Chapter 2

April 1990

"Hello, I'd like to speak to Mrs. Shaw." The oversized store detective stated.

"Speaking." Mrs. Shaw said as she held the phone with her shoulder and began to roll her eyes with annoyance.

"My name is Angela Martin and I am a store detective here at Famous Barr. I have your daughter Melody Shaw here with me along with her friends Brandon Miller and Tara Alexander. I along with another co-worker caught these three individuals shoplifting in our department store."

Mrs. Shaw stopped the store detective in the middle of the explanation, "Lock her stupid ass up!" She spoke very calmly with aggression and hung up the phone.

Melody looked at Tara with a smirk as they could hear her mother hang up the phone ending the call.

All for Love

Angela Martin couldn't believe it. This was the first time that a parent wasn't pleading and begging her not to arrest or press charges on their child. Angela took a deep breath and looked at the three individuals in front of her. "Today is going to be what I am going to consider your lucky day. I am not going to call another parent because I am aware this is not you all's first rodeo. I am not going to lecture you on how and where this road will lead you. I have a far greater rewarding opportunity. I am going to just let you go and pray that you don't come to this store or any other store thinking you can just pick up stuff and not pay for it. Looking at you it appears that you have someone that actually care about you. They are just fed up with the shenanigans."

Melody glanced at Brandon and Tara. Brandon had relief written all over his face. He knew that Mr. and Mrs. Miller would have killed him through the phone had they received that type of call. Tara was the only one that was in the clear. She lived with her aunt and boosting was her way of life. Tara was the reason Brandon and Melody had the courage to take their shot at the five-finger discount in the first place. Melody's mother had warned her that Tara thieving ways was going to land in her jail and she was not coming to get her. Today that warning came to fruition.

Angela stood up and adjusted her belt around her plump waist. With a straight face she waved towards the door saying, "Let's go Salt 'n Pepa and Heavy D." She escorted them out the door and led them to a stairwell.

She opened the door at looked them over and with the most serious look on her face she said, "I never want to see you in this store again. Go be great! Be the Queens and King you were meant to be."

Brandon led the way down the steps. Tara and Melody didn't say a word as they followed them out the door. Once they made their exit they noticed a Taco Bell directly across the street. Brandon looked at his childhood friends, "Y'all hungry."

Brandon placed his order and the girls placed theirs. He paid for their meals. The workers handed them their drinks and they went to take a seat near the window of the restaurant. Melody sat next to Brandon and Tara sat alone on her side of the booth.

There was a brief moment of silence. Then Melody spoke, "My mom is going to be on all bullshit. Man, I don't even want to go to her house. Aye, but I nearly pissed myself when that flashlight cop said, let's go Salt 'n Pepa and Heavy D."

Brandon chuckled, "That was a little funny. I surely wasn't about to laugh. I could see that going in a different direction if we would have laughed. Her big ass would have some old crazy stuff like she wasn't no joke and she trying to crack them." Brandon took a sip of his drink, "Speaking of jokes, you know when can actually say it was a joke. I will tell your mother that was me disguising my voice."

All for Love

Tara smirked, "She ain't falling for that. Mrs. Shaw be on that bs for real. I remember that time Melody missed curfew and she was sitting with rollers in her head and a red robe. For a moment I thought she was Satan. Her eyes were rolling as she screamed, I don't know what you little gals think this is but ain't nothing open after twelve but legs. I wanted to say to Melody so bad, you want me to check this hoe."

They all laughed as the Taco Bell worker brought them their meals. They thanked the worker as he walked away.

Brandon and Tara stop eating their food. Melody was chewing aggressively with a smack taking place here and there. They began to watch Melody as she ate. Brandon slightly turned his head in Melody's direction, "Slow down homegirl. You got me over here nervous. You got me under the assumption that this may be your last meal."

Melody looked up and slowed down as she took her last bite before she spoke, "Dude, I haven't eaten all day and we I get home I'm going straight to my room. I going to be in their starving because I'm not coming back out until my mom's take her ass to work." Melody grabbed a napkin from the stack on the table. She wiped her hands off. She reached toward Brandon and tapped him on his round belly. "You slow down a bit because you can stand to miss a meal or three, Heavy D."

Teresa Seals

They all laughed again. Brandon grabbed his chin, "I'm one fine chocolate chubby dude though. I more like Chubb Rock than a Heavy D."

Tara smirked, "You cool and plus you smart. But, you keep hanging with us, folks going to think you have a little sugar in your tank."

Brandon thick lashes accented his eyes. He looked directly in Tara eyes. He knew Tara was jealous of he and Melody's friendship. He always tried to avoid arguing with her whenever she made slick comments. He rubbed his right hand over his deep dark ocean waves, "I fuck with bitches and you two broads help me get'em. I'd knock you down, but I wouldn't be able to get rid of you."

Melody sniggered, "T, you ain't ready for B."

Tara didn't find anything funny. It burned her up whenever Melody sided with Brandon. She already knew how this would play out if she entertained Brandon's conversation. She took a bite of her taco and sipped her drink after she swallowed. She didn't know why Brandon was even there with them. His parents gave him the world. He was the baby boy. His dad remarried once his first wife died. His siblings were fifteen years older than him or better. He had nephew and nieces his age. His mom was a school teacher and his dad was a mortician. She and Melody were on Spring Break. She didn't know

All for Love

if Brandon was on Spring Break because he went to a Catholic school that wasn't in the neighborhood.

They all stood up to throw their trash away. Melody looked at her friends at the door. As they exited headed to the bus stop, they saw their bus coming. They all took off running down the street to catch their bus. The driver saw them coming and waited for them. As they approached the bus door the driver opened the door. They hopped on the bus. Each of them heavily panting trying to catch their breath.

Tara placed her hand on her hair brushing it back in her ponytail. Melody watched Tara and assisted her making sure her hair was all in place. Melody admired Tara's soft silky hair. She always said that if she had hair like Tara she wouldn't have cut her off in the short Anita Baker style. Melody hated getting her hair washed and pressed. It was think but not smooth. The relaxer and cut were right up her alley.

"This is a hell of away to start off my Spring Break. I know my moms is about to be on my head all this week. I am not going to be able to do anything. She is going to work my ass like a step-child. I'll probably be washing walls and cleaning all her China." Melody shook her head and hung it low just thinking about how this was all going to pan out. "I know she is not going to give me any money to go skating now." Melody placed her left hand on her face. She was trying to contain herself. The tears fell anyway.

Teresa Seals

"I got you homegirl. If you can go, I'll pay your way." Brandon pulled the string on the bus as he saw their stop approaching.

They stood up in unison and approached the door to exit the bus. The bus stopped, and they made their exit. The bus got them from downtown to the northside of the city. Today the two blocks from the bus stop in which they stayed was closer than usual. Melody was carrying a heavy burden. This was the third time her mother had received one of those calls from a department store. Tara and Brandon didn't know the exact amount of the wrath that Mrs. Shaw could bring but Melody burdens was theirs. If they could help her carry it, they would. That's just how tight they both were with Melody. They slowly dragged as they reached their block.

Tara stayed at the top of the street at the second house from the corner. Melody stayed in the middle of the block. Brandon stayed two houses from Melody. Tara stood on her porch watching her friends traveling to their designated areas. Melody waited until she seen her friends walk in their homes.

Melody knew Tara wouldn't have to go through any of the drama that awaited her on the other side of the door. Tara stayed with her aunt and cousins. Tara's mom would visit every now and then. She followed any man that payed her any attention. Brandon parents would have probably just told him not to do it again and

All for Love

increased his allowance, so he wouldn't go out stealing. They probably would go as far as giving him a credit card to ensure he wouldn't partake in that boosting lifestyle. Melody took a deep breath and pulled her door key out of her pocket. She opened the door and noticed black trash bags sitting at the door.

Mrs. Shaw came to door looking like Shug Avery in the *Color Purple,* "Call your granddaddy. They are waiting on you. I would take you myself but for the sake of my freedom, I'll let them come pick you up."

Weekends at grandmas became Melody's permanent place of residence in a matter of hours. Melody thought about the first time she went to stay with her grandparents. She was in the fifth grade. A tragic incident occurred in her fifth-grade class. Well, it was tragic the way she explained it to her mom. Her fifth-grade teacher Ms. Fisher took the rattan stick and popped her is what she said happened. However, as they were lining up Melody asked a girl in front of her what type of soap was did she used because she smelled good.

"Zest." She said.

Melody was pulled because at the time all she knew about was Dial soap. Melody repeated her, "Zest? Can you spell it?"

Ms. Fisher had been calling her little Alexis. This teacher just so happened to have been Melody's mother teacher along with her two uncles. Ms. Fisher stood with her salt and pepper afro in front the class dressed as though she was going to church and yelled out, "Little Alexis, I know your ass not talking in my line." She grabbed her rattan and began to head to the end of line where Melody was as she continued to speak, "Don't make me beat your tail to get you quiet."

The entire class was looking at Melody. She never replied when Ms. Fisher would call her by her mother's name but today was different. Melody stood on the opposite side of the line of Ms. Fisher.

"I don't know what type of student my mom was, but one thing for sure and two things for certain; I won't be the one getting my ass whopped. You put that stick on my and today will be the last day you lay hands on someone for talking."

All eyes were on Ms. Fisher. Her only reply was go to the principal's office. The principal called Mrs. Shaw. He let her know that Melody was not in any trouble, but she needed to pick her up. When Melody's mom came to the school Melody already had her version ready. When the principal said Ms., Fisher is Ms. Fisher and she hasn't changed. Melody was conjuring up more of her version. They made it to the door and Melody plan was in progress.

"Ma, what type of teacher was Ms. Fisher? Did she hit the and pinch the students? No, did she blow her nose and call the students to throw her tissue away?" Melody waited on her mother to respond.

All for Love

"You are not coming back here! You are going to go to that school by your granny's house."

It was easier than she expected. She was done with Ms. Fisher, but she had to stay with her grandparents. She had a few opportunities to come home during the week but when her dad had a job assignment in Nashville, Tennessee she was permanently at her grandparents for three months.

Melody looked at the black trash bags. She was glad that she didn't have to be confined to her room. She was more grateful that her mom didn't do anything physical to her. She didn't know why she pushed it to the limit because her mom didn't play about the disrespect. She called her buddies and let them know she had survived. They talked everyday of the week of Spring Break. She told them she wasn't going out the house until school. She wanted her grandmother and grandfather to see an angel and not a street runner. Street runner was the term she heard her mother use very often to describe her when ever she was on the phone. Brandon told her that he was going to work on getting his permit, so he and Tara would have some transportation to see their buddy.

Monday morning came, and her grandmother fixed her breakfast. When she was done with breakfast her grandfather was ready to take her to school. She let her grandfather know she would catch the bus back home. He agreed. Melody didn't think it was going to be too bad living with her dad's parents again. They always

Teresa Seals

treated her as though she was royalty. She was the only girl. They had raised two boys. Melody was that baby girl they always wanted. Although, she got this treatment when she visited them on the weekends, she just missed it because she didn't come visit as often as she did when she was younger. Of course, when school was over her first day at her new residence she walked home with Tara.

"I'm going to chill with you and Brandon for about an hour before I hop on this bus and go home. "Melody said to Tara as they sat on her front porch.

"Brandon should be walking around the corner any minute. I'm going to see if he wants to catch the bus with you to make sure you make it safely." Tara said thinking about her friend being by her lonely.

"Girl, you know Brandon's mom don't play that on a school night. He's going to have to do his homework before he can even come back out." Melody said as she snickered.

"All this over some damn Ralph Lauren." Tara said as she thought about their little Famous Barr escapade. "I got you caught up on my mission. Your family keeps you fly. I think I should just go talk to her, so she can just let you come back home."

"Girl, the hell you will. She would never let me live that down. She will be real reckless with that one. I can hear her now talking about you little follower the

All for Love

leader ass broad. I be ready to fight my momma." Melody shook her head just thinking about all the drama that would take place if Tara attempted to take up for her. "It's about to get dark. I need to get home before my grandmother be looking for me. Tell B I tried to wait. I'll call you when I make it home."

Tara stood up, "I'll walk you to the bus stop. I need to chill. You are right across the park. I'm acting like your way across town. It's just different not being able to walk right across the street your house I'm having a problem with."

"Yeah, I can catch this 42 Sarah and it puts me just about two blocks away from my grandparents. It's cool. I just got to find out my grandparent's rules. You know things change when it more than a weekend. Being in ninth grade is a lot different from fifth grade."

The buses ran every fifteen minutes. The bus to take Melody approached. Her grandparents were a five to seven-minute drive from her home and it took about forty-five minutes to an hour if you were walking. Melody exited the bus and began to walk towards her grandparent's street. As she approached the corner she could see a group of boys sitting on the porch of the corner house. Just as she was about to turn the corner she heard on of the boys call her name. She stopped and turned to look back. She noticed Benjamin approaching her. He was with a group some guys she recognized from school. He was swaged out looking like an Ice Cube knock off in his all black Raider's attire.

Teresa Seals

Melody was grinning from ear to ear. She had been crushing on him every since she and Tara had start going to church. He was looking totally different from the dude she always saw sound asleep on the church pew. She thought about the day she saw him. She almost didn't go but she was glad that Tara convinced her to go. She had been going to church every Sunday and seeing Benjamin was a hit or miss. He spoke to her one Sunday and she almost lost it. Just like she was about to lose it as she watched him as he approached her.

"Where you headed to Melly-Mel?" he asked.

Melody looked him over. The sun light hit his light brown eyes and she was caught up in his rapture, "I stay over here now and about to head in and do some homework."

"Homework? You don't even have no bookbag." He laughed, "Do you have anything you can take my number down?"

Melody pulled a folded-up piece of paper from her front pocket and an ink pen from her back pocket. She handed it to him with a matter fact look. She watched as he wrote on the paper. He handed it back to her. She looked it over.

"Brick? Why they call you that?" she was waiting on him to say his long ass name.

All for Love

"Cause I'm solid." He patted his chest.

"I'll call you later. I have to head on in this house and make sure my grandparents straight." Melody walked off from him blushing. Brick stood there as she walked up the street to the fourth house from the corner. He trotted his way back across the street and met back up with his friends.

Melody wanted to look back to see what he was doing but she noticed her grandmother standing in the door. She approached the door and looked back down the street to see if her grandmother could have possibly seen her talking to the young man. She didn't know what she would say but she knew if her mother would have seen her talking to him, she would have come out the bag with some of the wall stuff as if they were standing there undressing as they talked.

"How was your day?" Margie asked in a nice subtle way.

Melody let her know it was cool and she just missed her friends. Her grandmother let her know that maybe they could come over during the weekend. She'd ask James to go pick them up on Saturday after they left the grocery store.

Melody walked to the kitchen and picked up the receiver to the rotary phone. Her grandmother followed.

Teresa Seals

"James and I bought you a cordless phone. We know how you teenagers are these days. We hadn't had a phone in this room since your dad and uncle moved out. The socket is behind that dresser. I reckon it still works." Margie stood watching as Melody went to hook up the new gadget.

Her grandparents had been retired since she was in fifth grade. They didn't do much during the day but go see Margie's mother in the nursing home during the week and go to the grocery store on Saturday mornings. They may have drove to local restaurants when Margie didn't cook but that wasn't often. James would get up every morning, get dressed, ate breakfast and went to sit on the front porch to people watch until about lunchtime. Margie prepared three meals a day and sometimes desserts were included. Cakes, cookies and pies could be on the menu. When she pulled out that red and white Betty Crocker cook book there's no telling what type of dessert you would get. It was guaranteed to be delicious whatever it was she prepared.

Margie stood waiting to see if the phone would work. She had regular phones with cords. When she went to get the phone, she let the worker know it was for her teenage granddaughter. The clerk recommended the cordless phone.

"I have to let it charge before I will know if works." Melody said as the smell from the kitchen smacked her in the face, "Grammie what you cook?"

All for Love

"Go in there and see." Margie waved her hand as she straightened the dresser back up. She had a major case of OCD. Everything was always in place when you walked in her home. She cleaned as she cooked and as soon as everyone at she'd wash dishes and put the away. It was never a dirty dish to wake up to.

Melody ate and ran her bath water. She knew by the time she finished doing all her errands her cordless phone would have some juice. She went to her closet. Her grandmother had hung up some items and put the rest of her items in the dresser and chest in her room that once belong to her dad and uncle. The furniture was old, but it was clean and well kept. On the dresser was her parent's prom picture. She moved it behind the lamp because her mom appeared to be staring at her as she sat on the end of the bed.

Melody grabbed the phone. She already knew she wasn't going to be long. She had gotten sleepy suddenly. She called Brandon. He clicked over and put Tara on a three call. Brandon let them know he had football practice and that's why he didn't come home at his usual time.

Melody let them know that her grandmother said it was cool for them to come over on the weekend. Melody let them know that her grandparents went grocery shopping around nine in the morning and after they go to the nursing home to see her great-grandmother Sarah their day was done.

Teresa Seals

Melody got off the phone with Brandon and Tara. She grabbed the paper that Brick wrote put his number on. She dialed the number when the pulse beeped she noticed it was a pager number. She was not about to put her number in and wait on him to call her back. She didn't want him asking who this is and all the riggeromo that came when you paged someone. She decided to call her friend boy, Rasheed. He was someone she talked to on the phone. He'd ride down her mom's block and hop and chit chat. He was in deep relationship with the streets. He had broads. His blue BMW attracted them. He didn't sit by the phone often but when he did he had good conversation. By Melody's surprised he was home. She let him know her new location and the reason that landed it her there. He let her know that the next time she needed to go shopping it would be on him. She agreed and ended the call.

Made in the USA
Middletown, DE
07 July 2019